The Insect Se

© Gareth Lloyd 2022

To Saskia and Hannah, the two most beautiful people in my life.

AUTHOR'S NOTE: This story is set in Paris in the late 1980s, before the introduction of the Euro currency in France. The currency back then was French francs. 10 francs was worth around £1 or €1.3 or $1.5.

Chapter 1

When Alex Amis was young, no more than 20, he killed a man.

Why, he cannot honestly say. But, and this may surprise you, it was the beginning of a better, happier life for Alex.

He wasn't proud of what he did or the way he did it, but it freed him of so many of the conventions we are all taught to comply with before we're old enough to think for ourselves. The rules that seek to imprison us in conformity and that, for good and bad, hinder us from living the life we would want. The rules that until then had shackled him too.

Every person of that age goes through perhaps the most tumultuous phase of their life, as they transition from adolescence into adulthood. But this was anything but 'a phase of growing up' that people still like to say. It was Alex deciding to be the opposite of who he had been. To do something he could never have imagined doing, to act on impulse, and to see whether this could permanently change his own idea of who he was.

He was self-conscious to a degree that was far beyond the clichéd image of an introvert. For example, he'd never dance in a disco, thinking everybody would be looking at him. He'd never talk to people at parties, as he hated small talk. And when he couldn't avoid speaking to people, he struggled to move on from trivial subjects to those that really interested him, like literature, philosophy, music and film.

He was often described as a highly intelligent but socially inept young man.

His 'rebirth', such as he saw it, started on a typical weekend when he would walk around Paris, marvelling at the architecture that was, by decree, uniform in the façades of the city's residential buildings. This is what gives Paris an architectural coherence that greatly appealed to him.

Paris is greatly at odds with London, where stark skyscrapers stand alongside centuries-old buildings, often hiding some of the city's most appealing older buildings behind their modernist steel and glass facias.

Like Rome, Madrid, Lisbon and probably most historic cities, Paris has many secret treasures hidden in little known backstreets, often just a few hundred steps from their major tourist sites. Just a few steps could take you from the bustle of the city to almost silent streets and alleys seemingly lost in time.

It was in one such place that Alex committed what people say is an unforgivable crime, though he never accepted what he did as that. Ironically what he did that day was more like a caterpillar turning into a beautiful butterfly.

It was a bright spring day afternoon, with the first flower buds tentatively emerging from the previously frozen, then rainstorm muddied lawns of Le Jardin de Luxembourg.

Every time Alex ventured into central Paris from the City University on its outskirts, he would be sure to walk in these beautiful gardens. You'll find them near Paris' vibrant Latin Quarter, a haven of tranquillity amid the bustle all around it.

To walk there is like going back in time to the Paris of the 18 and 19th centuries, where lace frocked nannies would push their precious charges in steel framed prams, hoping to lull them to sleep in this rare oasis of greenery. These gardens are part of the opulent 'Rive Gauche' area, the left bank of the gently flowing Seine River that bisects the city.

From the Jardin de Luxembourg it was a mere few minutes by foot to the Latin Quarter and the Boulevard St. Michel, which leads to L'ile de la Cité. Here stands the Cathedral of Notre Dame, magnificent and imposing and seemingly protected by the huge statues of two horsemen in the square on which it had been built.

To reach this island that sat squarely in the middle of the Seine, Alex would always cross the Pont de St. Michel, near the famous Shakespeare and Company book shop. On occasion he would stop to browse some of his favourite French writers, such as Gide, Camus and Sartre. They were the famous existentialists whose works were part of Alex's Degree course.

At such a transitional age it is not surprising that people like Alex were drawn to the existentialist philosophy that insists we live in a world without God. We are simply creatures that exist, along with billions of others, for no divine reason or purpose. This means we must fashion our own morals and actions and take responsibility for whatever actions the course of our lives leads us to do.

These authors' views on life, death and morality had a profound effect on Alex, who had never read books of such depth growing up. And all the more so as he was a young man trying to understand life and his place in it.

The thoughts they expressed so beautifully are what, perhaps, sowed the seeds in his mind that led to him committing the act that day that led to such a seismic shift in his personality.

Because for all Alex's love of these remarkable books, he had always had a problem with a sentence in Camus' book 'The Plague' where it states that "There are more things to admire in men than to despise."

This was one of the few areas where Alex couldn't agree. His upbringing had shown him this, whether it was bullying at school, snide nicknames from his work colleagues in his holiday jobs and the general indifference to him from other students at his university.

Despite such experiences, Alex had always trusted in the honesty and decency of others. This persisted even though he continued being left disappointed when, again and again, his trust was proven to be misplaced. This had given him a sense of wearied sadness at the way that people and the world really worked. Being honest, which he always felt was his guiding moral, seemed to encourage others to exploit his good nature.

It could be argued that it was his built-up resentment at what he saw as the hypocrisy of so many people, that led him to an act that demonstrates how easy it is for good people to do bad things.

Chapter 2

To cross to the right side of the city, 'la rive droite', Alex continued straight to the Pont au Change, another famous Parisian landmark. In Patrick Süskind's 'Perfume', this was the location of the detestable perfumier Giuseppe Baldini's shop that fell into the Seine drowning him and everything he owned once the book's anti-hero had finally escaped Baldini's greedy clutches.

This reference to Perfume is perhaps appropriate because something, maybe a smell carried on the wind, drew Alex to a part of the city he had never explored. There were ancient cobbled streets and bridge arches. They seemed drawn from a Charles Dickens or Victor Hugo novel, where the poorest inhabitants of the city would conjugate to buy food from the sprawl of carts lined up in filth ridden streets, or to protest at the injustices of their lives.

Passing through one of these stone arches Alex found himself lost, but wonderfully so, in a road of strange and ancient looking boutiques, one of which by chance he entered.

He was staggered by what he saw. Mounted on the walls of the shop were glass cases wherein were arranged insects of all natures. There must have been thousands of them, each neatly held in place by a single pin, their bodies conserved in a macabre display. Butterflies, dragonflies, spiders and bugs adorned all the walls, their corpses remarkably preserved in a show of different colours quite overwhelming to the senses.

After his initial amazement, something fundamental shifted inside him, giving way to a wave of disgust. These creatures had all lived, but none to their full term. They had been killed to sell to entomologists, who no doubt would compete with fellow collectors to boast about their latest acquisition.

Surely these people weren't oblivious to the fact that each specimen had been killed then had a pin thrust through their thorax simply to satisfy some strange pleasure of theirs? Of course they knew but they simply didn't care. Was such a small aspect of their lives really worth the deaths of so many thousand other lives on the planet we share with them?

Alex's eye was drawn to what was undoubtedly the prize exhibit in this abominable establishment. It was a huge beetle, larger than the size of his hand, encased in a polished mahogany box.

Its thorax was as black as night on the left side and as white as the stars on the other. By nature Alex was not fond of insects, but this beetle was one of the one most stunningly beautiful examples of what Nature is capable of that he had ever seen.

"We're closing" a voice called out, and not in a pleasant way. It was only then that Alex noticed a bearded, bored-looking man sat behind the shop counter watching a small TV set.

"Buy now or leave", he continued in his charmless way. As there were no other people in what was clearly his shop, he directed his words and an unfriendly gaze directly at Alex.

This further roused his anger that had already been heightened by the sight of this shrine to murder.

'This beetle," he said. "May I take a closer look?"

The shop owner sighed and said "Only if you're quick about it. I have to a wife to get home to and a supper of whatever she's cooked up to eat this time."

It seemed the man had as much respect for his wife as he did for his customers.

Alex carefully took the box from the wall, which naturally raised a look of great approbation from the shop owner. And just as he was about to complain, Alex smiled and said "I'll take it."
At once the shopkeeper's demeanour changed. In his eyes, Alex had transformed himself from a

time waster to a valued customer about to buy his most expensive item.

"A wonderful choice, sir" he said as Alex approached the counter with the box. "Very rare, very beautiful and, as you can imagine, very expensive. But a great investment too. I assume you know how rare these creatures are?"

"Indeed," Alex nodded, looking at the exorbitant price tag. "And I have a question…"

"Yes sir?", replied the shopkeeper, feigning a politeness all so obviously contrived given his behaviour up to that point.

Alex moved his arm across the shop, just like a magician's assistant might at the end of a particularly impressive illusion.

"Why?" he simply said.

The shopkeeper looked at Alex, confused. "Why what?"

"Why kill all these creatures? Is it just to bolster the pride of other entomologists in their morbid collections?"

Clearly he had never been asked this question because he stared at Alex as if he was after all the idiot he had assumed when this man had entered his little empire.

He shrugged his shoulders and stared intensely into Alex's eyes.

"Why? Because I can".

"And how do your children feel about what you do?"

"I don't have any," he replied gruffly. "These are my children."

"So you surround yourself with dead children?"

"If you're not interested then please leave my shop. I don't have time for people who waste mine."

An uncomfortable silence ensued, broken by Alex asking "Can you gift wrap it? I know someone who would love to receive a dead beetle for their birthday. They're strange that way."

The shopkeeper let out a breath of air in frustration. "So you don't like what I do, but you want to buy what I sell."

He clearly wanted this day to end, but not so much that he'd miss out such a lucrative last sale.

"Do you speak to all your customers this way? I'm sure I can find my friend something else, somewhere else for the 6,000 francs you're charging for this."

"No sir, please don't leave. I sincerely apologise if I have insulted you in any way. Let me look for some suitable wrapping paper for your friend."

As he sorted through the mass of brown paper he would normally use to wrap purchases, he finally and triumphantly raised something resembling gift paper. But his smile froze in horror as he saw Alex's arms stretched up towards the ceiling still holding the mahogany encased exhibit.

He sent the box crashing down onto the shopkeeper's head, shards of glass scattering in all directions. Such was the force, the beetle escaped the pins that had held it the box for who knows how long.

Then a surprisingly large gushing of blood ran from the shop keeper's neck, where Alex could see a large shard of glass has imbedded itself. Clutching at his now crimson soaked neck the man sank to the floor, his eyes still staring at Alex, only this time in disbelief.

Even though Alex had not intended to kill him, he felt nothing. Not anger, not remorse, not even shock at what he had just done. Nothing at all but perhaps the waning of his disgust at the dead man and his sordid little shop. For the first time in his life he had acted on his instincts, believing – for right or wrong – that all creatures should be seen as equal. That no life was worth more than any other.

Aware his life was rapidly ebbing away as blood soaked through his shirt, the shop owner gurgled his last words.

"But why?"

Alex shrugged his shoulders.

"Because I can."

Then he turned and left the shop, but not before taking the beetle and putting it in his coat pocket.

CHAPTER 3

The heavy doors of the La Santé prison creaked opened and a large, black figure emerged, clutching a plastic bag of what few possessions he owned.

"Goodbye and good luck Brutus," said the guard, who for the first years of the man's prison sentence had tried to provoke him to violence with insults about his colour and background ("fucking black bastard", "immigrant scum" etc), but who had slowly learnt to admire this prisoner's calm resolve and impeccable behaviour.

"Normally I say 'see you again soon' to prisoners on release, but something tells me you won't be back here, Brutus."

He even extended his hand. "No hard feelings, eh?"

"Farewell" replied Brutus shaking his hand with minimal conviction as he breathed in the air of freedom for the first time in seven years.

Even though he had exercised frequently in the prison yard, breathing in the same air, it was so much sweeter now he was finally outside those hated walls.

There was no welcoming party outside the prison. That was at Brutus' request. He simply turned his feet towards the centre of Paris and started walking, smiling at what he was going to do now, and to whom.

CHAPTER 4

Brutus was the nickname he had acquired in prison through his size and strength. He was, or rather had been, a feared drug dealer on the infamous Rue St. Denis. No-one dared cross him, such was his reputation for extreme retribution if they did.

No-one, that is, except a young and ambitious police officer by the name of César Dumal. He had framed Brutus for the murder of a woman Brutus didn't even know, and who he had soon deduced Dumal himself must have killed.

He was right. Dumal had himself shot the woman on the orders of her husband, a magistrate who had fallen for another, much younger woman. What the magistrate would have lost in assets when she divorced him would dwarf the 200,000 francs he had agreed to pay Dumal to make the problem go away.

It was well known in the higher echelons of Paris society that 'delicate problems' such as the magistrate's could be resolved by this policeman, provided the price was right.

Anonymity on both sides was of course essential, so before meeting any client Dumal would insist on talking to them though a separate phoneline in his apartment.

He would record the conversation, and make it very clear he was doing so, in case any client should ever refuse to pay for his work or renege on their vow of silence. Payment had always to be made in cash too, for the safety of both sides.

Dumal would simply ask what needed doing, name his price (based largely on how wealthy he knew the client was) and where he could find the target when he or she was alone.

In Brutus' case, Dumal had used one of his favourite techniques to ensure a conviction.

He first called into the wife's house, his police uniform convincing her he offered no danger. Once she had let him in, and turned her back, he shot her twice in the head. He used one of several unregistered pistols he'd surreptitiously taken from crime scenes over the years.

He then put the gun back in his pocket, and unholstered his service pistol. He then grabbed any jewellery he could see and the money in her handbag, before running into the road screaming at the bystanders that he was police and for them to move out of his way.

He would head straight for the first black or Asian man he could see. Brutus just happened to be the wrong man in the wrong place at the wrong time.

As those in the street scattered at the sight of a policeman brandishing a gun, Dumal shot Brutus directly in the chest. Kneeling to handcuff the prostrate figure, he made sure no onlookers could see him placing the murder weapon in Brutus' hand as he lay there bleeding out – and placing pieces of the dead woman's jewellery in his trouser pocket.

In the general confusion and panic, no-one saw this. They never did. They simply saw a hero cop who had potentially saved their lives from a black man with a gun and who was now desperately trying to save the man he had just shot.

Racism in France at that time was endemic and most people saw all immigrants as criminals or spongers off the state. So no-one could possibly suspect Dumal of using excessive force to take down this dangerous man.

Dumal had expected Brutus to die quickly, and had taken off his officer jacket in a pretence of pressing it against the chest wound to stem the blood pouring from it. But in reality he was applying no pressure on it at all, just waiting for Brutus to die. He shouted for someone to call an ambulance.

A few minutes later, an ambulance and two police cars screeched to a halt beside them. Dumal swore to himself at their promptness, realising someone on the street must have called for help the moment they heard gun shots. Dumal left the paramedics to take over, as they hurriedly checked his pulse, administered oxygen and put Brutus in the back of their ambulance.

Brutus looked close to death, with a far-off stare in his eyes and Dumal was satisfied he'd be pronounced dead on arrival at the hospital. But somehow the bullet had missed all his vital organs and he was saved.

But not from imprisonment.

When questioned about the killing, Dumal claimed he had heard pistol shots and seen Brutus running from a building. He then pursued him on foot before shooting him as he tried to lose Dumal on the street.

Despite having no obvious motive to kill the murdered woman and no trace of gunpowder residue on his hands, Brutus had a long list of previous convictions for burglary, drug dealing and violence. With his fingerprints on the murder weapon, his proximity to the murder scene and the dead women's jewellery in his pocket, the jury took less than 2 hours to condemn him.

He was sentenced to fourteen years imprisonment while Dumal was hailed as a hero for having risked his life to arrest the murderer. Soon after he received a medal for valour.

CHAPTER 5

Brutus was tough when he entered La Santé prison, but he was even more formidable when he left.

Despite multiple provocations from the guards and other prisoners, he had been a model inmate, working hard, attending whatever pointless courses on anger management they arranged for the prisoners, and quickly obeying any order from the guards.

He even ran an exercise programme for his inmates to help them stay fit and bulk up to something approaching his size and physique. His behaviour was so exemplary he received release on parole after just 7 years of his sentence.

But while he had seemed to manage his emotions well inside the jail, he had been concentrating them into a fury against the detective who had done this to him. He had even decided how he would make Dumal pay dearly for what he had done when he was released.

And now he was free.

CHAPTER 6

Inspector César Dumal was not a good man. And most definitely not an honest one. But since his framing of Brutus he had become one of the most powerful police officers in the city. He was a Brigadier of the Paris Police, to give him his proper, rather grandiose title that is so often given to people who serve their country at any elevated level.

Dishonesty isn't particularly rare in any police force, but Dumal combined it with the particularly vicious streak he had long displayed.

When aged just six he had hit his mother simply for refusing him a biscuit. At 8 he dropped the new family puppy from a third floor window 'to see what would happen'. It died instantly. And at 11 he pushed a pupil into the school's swimming pool because he knew the kid couldn't swim. He laughed as his victim flayed wildly trying to stay above the surface.

Fortunately a lifeguard was on hand to save the child, and he reported the incident to the School Head.

Any other pupil would have been expelled immediately from such a prestigious private school. But Dumal's parents, his father a surgeon, his mother an eminent architect, were affluent enough to be patrons of the school, who depended on gifts such as theirs to maintain their excellent facilities and so attract new pupils.

The incident was therefore hushed up as an unfortunate accident and Dumal continued at the school as before, only now with an even greater sense of invulnerability.

Other pupils feared him as they knew if he could go unpunished from almost drowning one of them, he could do anything. Needless to say, he used their fear to begin extorting money, food and any clothes he liked from them, learning the lessons of intimidation that would continue into his adulthood.

His parents initially hoped he would follow in their footsteps and have a successful professional career. But they soon realised César was too lazy to apply himself sufficiently to academic study.

He was always looking for short cuts to get what he wanted and felt entitled to. After all, he thought, why slog away for 30 years for money when you can intimidate weaker people to give it to you in less than half that time?

This is why César decided that crime would be his best career path. He would make sure he had sufficient power to extort money from the lowest pimp to the great and the good of Paris, even though this would require far more serious threats, blackmail and dishonesty that he had learnt in his formative days at school.

Dumal wasn't intelligent, but he was smart enough to realise that the greatest danger to his plans of major extortion was arrest and imprisonment. The natural safeguard to this was to become a policeman himself. He could then lead investigations away from his involvement in anything suspicious, or to destroy key evidence linking him to it. Plus, he didn't need the good grades he had no chance of attaining to apply for the police force.

His parents were less than happy when he told them of his decision. They wondered how to explain this to their elevated circle of friends, who they knew would be laughing behind their back at their son's failure to follow a more distinguished, better paid career. They would be sure to hint at it, without directly ever saying it of course. For Dumal's parents, who had long lived in such society, this was one of the most humiliating things that could happen to them.

So César's parents decided to say, whenever asked about how their son's career was going, that they were very proud of him for putting his life on the line to protect honest citizens like them from the criminality in the city.

César had, they stressed, always loved to help people. He was now doing this professionally and, after all, wasn't his work more beneficial to society than that of their children, most of whom were now helping clients to avoid taxation or to overcome planning regulations, or defending the very worst murderers? It was a strategy that quickly shut down such conversations.

The reality was that, with their contacts, they knew they could elevate their son to a socially acceptable position in the force a lot quicker than the lower-class people the police usually drew their recruits from. Status to them was everything, and a senior police officer had always demanded respect in the class of people they counted as friends.

Deep down they also hoped the responsibility of civic duty and the strict rules regarding his actions might smooth out the impetuousness and cruelty they had witnessed so often throughout their son's childhood.

César had also been sure to make them feel guilty about how they had parented him. Their long hours at work meant he grew up largely in the care of various nannies or au pairs, who never felt they had the authority to curb the extreme behaviour he so frequently exhibited. If ever they mentioned this to his parents, César would accuse them of punishing him physically, even going as far as to bruise himself to show his parents what they had done. They would then be dismissed.

His parents only way of showing him love was to throw money at him. From his teens he had received a generous allowance, allowing him to buy everything an adolescent could want. The newest video consoles, the trendiest trainers and clothes, then as he grew older, cars always more expensive than his schoolmates could afford, or whose parents weren't foolish enough to buy for them.

So César grew up expecting the best of everything, regardless of how he behaved. He was nothing special to look at, but wearing expensive clothes partly made up for that. He was of less than medium height and build with a distinctive hawkish look to his face that did little to hide his predatory instincts.

It was a face that rarely hid his scorn for those around him, unless of course they could be of use. It then broke out into a beaming and reassuring smile, drawing them to him like a moth to a flame.

So, immediately after school, César became a cadet in the Paris police force. And despite his parents' concerns about his future, what mother wouldn't be proud to see her son, so smart in his uniform, working for the good of others?

CHAPTER 7

Safeguarding others was, of course, of no interest to Dumal. He set about straightaway on a path that would accelerate his rise among the force and the ever-greater protection this would afford to his illegal activities.

He made sure to cultivate good relationships with the city's dignitaries and powerbrokers, with many soon beholden to him for covering up their various indiscretions, frauds, corrupt deals and other crimes. As a result he was soon so well connected and protected that he felt free to do as he pleased.

With his ruthlessness, determination and the occasional subtle intervention from his parents, he rose quickly to the rank of Brigadier of the Paris Police Force. Such was his power that not even an acrimonious divorce, after his wife Chantal had accused him of domestic abuse (and had multiple bruises to prove it), raised an eyebrow at the Police Prefecture.

Their marriage had been a disaster. César had at first seemed perfect husband material, charming, ambitious and rising quickly through the police ranks. But once married, Chantal quickly realised his true nature. He would get angry should she ever disagree with him, and violent if she did so after he had been drinking.

The violence started with a few slaps but quickly escalated to punches, kicks and finally her being pulled by her hair through their apartment. It was after a particularly savage beating that she had finally escaped to a women's shelter who reported her husband to the police.

Dumal knew a conviction would spell the end of his career, and perhaps even time in jail. So when he realised his sugary sweet promises to never do it again were now falling on deaf ears, he instead went on the attack by ruining her reputation.

To explain her injuries, he swore she was a drunk and had fallen onto a lounge table. He even coerced friends of theirs to testify that his wife was indeed an alcoholic and that they had seen her collapse through drink several times before.

With his unblemished record, she was scorned for lying simply to get a larger divorce settlement. César even threatened to sue her for slander should she ever repeat her ridiculous allegations.

So it was to no-one's surprise that the case was dismissed before ever reaching a magistrate. In fact his stature in the force actually rose from evading so serious a charge.

Few of his colleagues believed in his innocence though, having themselves been on the wrong side of his fury in the past.

One result of this close shave with his now ex-wife was to make Dumal far more cautious in how he acted. He knew he would have to tread carefully if he was to ensure his plans for the far more lucrative work of extortion could be realised. This meant making sure he always had a scapegoat should things go seriously wrong.

He insisted on investigating any criminal case he had been involved in and might be linked to. To assist his 'clients' he thought nothing of tampering with evidence, framing innocent people like Brutus, threatening witnesses or, when absolutely necessary, bribing jury members to ensure a not guilty verdict.

Even those in the police force who suspected what he was doing were too afraid to speak up, knowing that he could and would destroy their careers for doing so.

Not surprisingly therefore, Dumal boasted by far the highest crime conviction rate in the whole of Paris. And no-one ever questioned how he'd achieved this, even though he seemed to always find the key evidence at the right time, despite seeming to do so little detective work.

Despite his rapid rise through the ranks, and his side takings from helping out those rich enough to afford him, Dumal soon realised that it would never be enough to pay for the early retirement he craved. He wanted the big money, despite the risks it carried.

From the beginning of his career, he had a clear goal in mind. This was to retire early to a house on the French Riviera, with a large balcony overlooking the Mediterranean. Especially he dreamed of sitting on a sun-soaked balcony where, with glass of ice cold champagne, he could look out over the sea and congratulate himself for creating the perfect life for himself. He cared not about the damage he would have to do to other people's lives to achieve this. It was, after all, what a man like him deserved.

His first idea was to fake the deaths of his parents for the large inheritance he would receive. Maybe a tragic accident, like a car crash, due to a sudden loss of brake fluid? Perhaps carbon monoxide poisoning from a faulty boiler? Maybe even assassination by a masked intruder. But none of this was possible as he would be an immediate suspect, and in a case that by law he'd be forbidden to investigate. He was, after all, surrounded by smarter, harder working detectives with every reason to convict him.

This, more than any love he felt for his parents, prevented him planning their sudden demise any further.

Instead he started to think how he could extort serious money from those he could easily control and who wouldn't dare stand up to him.

CHAPTER 8

Brutus had to find the man he hated the most of all of Paris. But first he had to visit the man he loved the most there too.

He made his way towards the Rue St. Denis, nodding back at those who still recognised him, or shouted out their congratulations to him on being finally released.

It was Pascal he most wanted to see. Pascal, his best friend from childhood. Pascal who had continued to protect his patch during those seven long years, still sharing half his proceeds, which he'd hidden for him. Pascal who had never missed a visiting hour, sent him letters every week and had smuggled money into La Santé to pay the guards to make sure nothing happened to his friend.

Pascal had wanted to pick him up from the prison, but Brutus had insisted he didn't. Pascal had a long police record too, and the two couldn't be seen together the minute Brutus was freed.

When Pascal saw Brutus walking towards him, his face broke into a huge smile. They hugged like long lost friends.

"Thank you, my brother," said Brutus. "Thank you for everything."

"For what?" laughed Pascal. "A bit of cash to keep the screws happy? It's a drop in the ocean compared to what we're making here. There's a new, powerful type of hash coming in that people are going crazy for. We're raking the money in."

As he said this, he stuffed a large wad of francs into Brutus' shirt pocket, patted it and handed him a key.

"You know where the apartment is. The spare room is ready for you, the address is registered with the parole board and you'll find new clothes on your bed. Now
go and get some sleep. The fridge is stacked too, so just help yourself my friend."

They hugged again and Brutus headed for the apartment which was on a small side street less than 300 metres away.

Brutus felt his eyes tearing up at the love and loyalty his friend had always shown him. But this was no time for sentiment. Those seven years that bastard Dumal had condemned him to had left little room for any other emotion than a burning desire for vengeance.

CHAPTER 9

Tonight, as on every Saturday night, it was time for Dumal to make the collections. This meant visiting every whore, pimp and drug dealer noted in the ledger the French Mafia had handed over to him, along with dates of payment, amounts paid and amounts due.

Dumal had to constantly update the ledger due to the many murders, convictions and personnel changes that occurred among the scum of Paris that worked the area.

This was easy enough for him though. These reprobates made practically no effort to hide their profession. So when one name disappeared it was simple to find the replacement and dictate to him the terms of his or her 'insurance policy' with Dumal.

If they wished to ply their filthy trade, they had to pay him. What they did then was of no concern to him, even though he knew the brothel owners catered for customers who would pay them large sums of money to satisfy the most depraved fetishes.

His patch, the Rue St. Denis, is a long and sordid street that starts close to the Gare du Lyon, but just hidden enough that the passengers disgorged throughout the day by Eurostar trains can't see it in all its sleazy magnitude.

Rue St Denis runs directly south to the tourist centre of Paris. Needless to say, the Paris Mafia were none too pleased to cede this prime extortion spot to Dumal. But one of the first things César had done upon becoming Brigadier of the Paris Police was to approach the crime bosses of the city with a powerful threat.

He explained that should they refuse his desire to take over protection for this one street, he would immediately raid all their brothels and crack dens in Pigalle, the main centre of vice in Paris, and their prime source of income.
Faced with what would be for them a huge loss in earnings, they grudgingly accepted. They knew all too well Dumal's reputation as a ruthless and corrupt policeman, who would carry out his threat immediately if they refused him.

He had turned down flat their offer of a huge bribe instead, as he knew it was a mere fraction of the money he would be extorting every week. He simply agreed to pay them the money they bribed the police each month to leave the operation alone. He, after all, could hardly do this, but would keep the rest of the cash.

They handed him their ledger book for the area, where the names of all the individuals and businesses they were receiving money from were listed. To save face, a matter very important to them, they insisted on his help in future should the need arise. The deal was a smart move in ensuring their own protection.

Dumal readily agreed, as this was, after all, his speciality. And indeed, on several occasions he was able to ensure clearly guilty members of their gangs walked free due to a technicality or a lack of evidence.

Dumal knew how dangerous it was to take on the French Mafia. But his lifelong use of extortion had shown him that it was a game of smoke and mirrors, where everyone had to seem more powerful than they really were.

Seeming weak to seasoned killers was never a good option and he knew the Paris Mafia would be following his actions to see how he ran their former business there. He therefore needed someone intimidating to do the hard graft for him. Someone who could not just scare those who paid him, but also to make it look like Dumal had a network of police officers they dare not risk going to war with.

Few police were as corrupt as Dumal, though, and many were genuinely incorruptible at any price. So he needed to find someone who was desperate for the extra money such work would provide.

He studied the backgrounds of the cops in his division and eventually found a heavy-set colleague called Jean who would fit the part perfectly.

Jean's wife had died early, leaving him with three kids to care for. This wasn't easy on a police officer's wage, so Jean gladly accepted his proposal.

Dumal couched this illicit work in terms of exacting a fee from those who thought they could defy law and order. Jean of course saw right through this, but played along to secure the extra income he needed to pay off his mounting rent arrears and credit card debts.

Dumal, with self-protection always in mind, usually had Jean making their collections. He was far more intimidating, being at least a foot taller, more muscular and with intimidating tattoos and scars on his arms. He looked more like a mafia enforcer than a policeman, which suited Dumal perfectly. He was the brains, Jean the brawn. And to those who paid them, what was the difference between paying the mafia or someone who was a corrupt police officer?

But tonight Jean was in hospital with a broken jaw, following an altercation with a new pimp on their turf who hadn't yet learnt the way things worked there. Ironically his assailant was in the same hospital, only with four broken ribs, a fractured jaw and a broken collarbone that Dumal had bestowed on him with a crowbar once he heard about the attack on his partner.

So that Friday afternoon it was Dumal himself who had to collect the payments. Changing from his work uniform to black trousers and a black hoodie to protect him from the unlikely event he was spotted, he followed his usual routine of taking the Metro to Strasbourg-St. Denis then descending Rue St. Denis on the left side before ascending it on the right so he could take the same journey home.

He always carried one of his unregistered pistols to carry out this work, just in case anything went wrong or someone dared to defy his demands.

He figured his route down and then up the street would remind those on each side that it was collection time, so they could count out the money ready for him. He had no desire to linger any longer than he needed in this repugnant area, where he himself might be at risk of attack from a new lowlife who didn't know who he was but might guess just how much money he would have collected.

All was going smoothly on his route until one dealer said he couldn't pay the weekly fee.

"Business is slow" he explained. "Customers are moving on to stronger weed and my supplier has been arrested."

Dumal consulted the ledger.

"That's not my problem. It's 4,000 francs or a beating. Your choice. Or I can put the police onto you and you can get a nice, long prison sentence."

"Please, I pay you double next week" the man pleaded.

Dumal pretended to consider this. But as he knew many of his other payees were watching this confrontation, he knew he couldn't be seen to be weak. He pulled out his pistol, aimed it at the dealer's head, then turned it round and cracked the butt into the man's temple.

This was not because of any generosity of spirit but because a murder there and then in front of so many eye witnesses would be difficult to cover up. There was always someone desperate enough to step forward and describe him to the investigating team if a reward was offered.

Even more importantly to Dumal, though, was that killing this upstart who had dared to default on his payment would almost certainly mean an unnecessary loss of earnings until a new reprobate took his place. And to Dumal, money always came first.

The pistol strike had floored the dealer, so Dumal knelt down beside him and snarled, loudly enough for the crowd to hear, "It's now 10,000 francs next week. Or I'll be using the other end of this pistol. Understand?"

The man nodded in scared submission, blood seeping down his neck.

"Get up and get working" shouted Dumal. "And remember, it's 10,000 francs next Saturday or your life".

Satisfied at his show of authority, and especially how the onlookers had recoiled when they saw his pistol and the blood flowing from the forehead of his victim, Dumal continued down the street. Once his business was finished, and his pockets filled with 200,000 francs, he headed back home from the same tube station towards his upmarket apartment less than 200 yards from the Rue de Rivoli.

This area would also be too expensive for a normal, honest inspector to afford. But Dumal didn't care about that. He'd extorted that night alone more than the annual cost of running his apartment, even though he'd have to split it with Jean. And if he was ever challenged about where he lived, he could simply explain his parents had given him a large deposit to help him buy it.

He knew they'd lie to protect him, such would be the disgrace of a conviction to them. Such is the way life works for those more privileged than most.

CHAPTER 10

Unfortunately for Alex, it would be Inspector Dumal who would investigate the murder he had committed.

It was just 20 minutes after he'd stashed that week's collection that Dumal got the phone call.

"Brigadier there's been a death at an entomologist's shop. Can you come and have a look at it?"

"Entomologist?"

"Insect collector, sir"

"Ah, entomologist, I must have misheard you" said Dumal always embarrassed when junior officers showed themselves more knowledgeable than him.

He took down the address and walked to the site, not half a mile from the building where he worked.

The shop was cordoned off, with most of the forensics team taking off their plastic clothes and shoe covers while others took photographs of the dead man.

"Anything?" asked Dumal to the two officers who were carefully studying the body.

"Nothing, sir. No prints on the case, other than the shopkeeper's, no forced entry, nothing stolen."

He returned to the murder scene while the other officer continued.

"There is a bump on his head but it wasn't caused by a sharp object. We'll know more after the autopsy but my guess is that he accidentally dropped the wooden case, which to be fair is surprisingly heavy, onto his head while holding it up and the shattered glass fell on him. That would certainly explain how the glass ended up where it did. He has multiple lacerations on his upper body and, of course, the large shard in his neck, but otherwise no visible bruising on his body. There are no signs of a struggle either. So I'd say it looks a lot more like an accident than murder or suicide."

"Who found the body?"

"A couple passing by noticed the lights were on and tried the shop door. They found it was open and then saw the body lying in a pool of blood. The door being unlocked seemed strange to them of course, but this further suggests an accident, as a dead shopkeeper couldn't lock it. We've got a statement from the couple and their address if you need to talk to them but they are just a normal couple walking home from dinner at a restaurant. We've checked the restaurant and they were definitely there at the time we predict the death took place."

"Prints on the door handle?"

"Multiple prints sir, but then again this is a shop."

"Is it really," Dumal answered sarcastically.

Behind the officer, Dumal could see the blood, shards of glass and the foot of the dead man. He walked over to survey the scene.

"So, a shard of glass through the neck. Not how I'd choose to go."

"It's very odd, sir."

"No kidding," muttered Dumal. "Do we know approximate time of death?"

"Only a couple of hours or so ago, according to initial forensics, so around 6pm sir. That happens to be when the shop closes."

The other officer returned.

"And what was in the display cabinet?"

The two looked at each other and shrugged.

"We've found nothing sir. We didn't think to look. We assumed it was a new cabinet or one he had just opened to sell whatever it contained. Perhaps it was a new one not yet used."

"Like those over there perhaps," sighed Dumal pointing towards the wall where identical cabinets were displayed. Only one was missing.

"Oh" was all the two officers could say.

"If you're thinking of sitting the detective exam anytime soon, I don't fancy your chances. Look for what was in that case. Look everywhere. For all we know he could have been killed for that alone. If you find nothing, put out an appeal for anyone who was in the shop around the time of his death."

The officers nodded.

Dumal was less than pleased he had a new case to investigate. These things took up valuable time. Time better spent amassing extra money for his house on the Mediterranean.

"What was the name of the deceased?" he sighed.

"Xavier Deschamps"

"Any family?"

"Yes sir, a wife, Marie. We're getting her address now. Do you want me to break the news to her?"

"No, leave that to me. I'm used to giving bad news to people."

CHAPTER 11

Brutus was keeping a deliberately low profile. He suspected the police would check he hadn't gone straight back to being one of the main drug dealers on the Rue St. Denis.

He stayed in Pascal's apartment for a few days, savouring his freedom, telling Pascal tales of his time in jail, visiting his parole officer and seemingly behaving like the fully reformed citizen that such a long stretch in prison was supposed to have made him.

He got a job in a fast food restaurant, making his parole officer even happier to the degree that he sensed Brutus truly was reformed. Such was the workload of a Parisian parole officer, he soon let Brutus reduce his visits to just once a month.

But all the time Brutus was thinking of HIM. That man who had stolen 7 years of his life and what he would do once he caught up with him.

Unfortunately for Brutus, Pascal didn't realise it was Dumal who had made the most recent collection. It was Jean's face that Pascal knew. The guy who had come that last Saturday he assumed was just another mafia thug, no doubt sent in place of the other one, who could be dead for all he knew.

He had heard this new guy say something about the police but hadn't caught all of it. The Police, The Mafia, it made no difference to Pascal. They were all the same.

Pascal's name was in that ledger, and he too had handed over the 4,000 francs as usual. If only he had known this man wasn't just police, but the very man his friend was looking for, he could have saved Brutus so much time and effort.

Dumal had escaped justice for now. But when the time came it would be a very different kind of justice.

After a week of rest, Brutus took the large stash of cash Pascal had accumulated for him. He then rented a small room at an extortionate price in direct sight of the police commissariat where he knew Dumal worked.

Whenever his job allowed, he would study the comings and goings into the building using high powered binoculars to see the people in their cars. But he never once caught sight of his prey.

One day he even tried standing by the entrance to see better into the car windows of the vehicles that entered, and asking those entering on foot where he might find Brigadier Dumal. But no-one even answered him, scurrying inside no doubt just because of the colour of his skin.

Then one day, finally, he spotted Dumal driving into the commissariat in a sleek, black Audi. He hadn't aged nearly as much as Brutus. But then their lives had hardly been the same.

Brutus noted down the number plate then lay back in his attic room, smiling.

"I've got you now," he said quietly to himself.

CHAPTER 12

A few hours after visiting the crime scene at the insect collector's shop, Brigadier Dumal knocked at the door of Marie Deschamps house in the upmarket area of Monceau.

She answered the door and was surprised to see an officer of the law standing there. But not as surprised as Dumal was at Marie's beauty. He checked the door number again. Was she really the wife of that fat, aged and bloodless corpse he had just examined? If so, he must have had a lot of money if he could afford a three storey home in this area of Paris and a wife as attractive to match. She must have married him for his money he thought..

"Marie Deschamps?"

"Yes."

"I'm Brigadier Dumal of the Paris Police. May I come in? I'm afraid I have some bad news"

Marie's face went pale as she let the officer into the hallway.

"Is it my husband? Is he OK? I was expecting him home a while ago."

Dumal looked down at his shoes in a pretence of sympathy

"It is Madame. I'm afraid your husband is dead. He was found in his shop earlier this evening with significant facial injuries. Either it was suicide, a freak accident or murder. We are investigating and I will, of course, keep you fully updated."

Marie turned away and started sobbing.

"Xavier would never have killed himself."

Dumal handed her a tissue, taking the opportunity to get a fuller view of her delicious body as she pressed it to her eyes.

"Did Xavier have any enemies?"

"No. Or at least none that I know of. He spent most of his time in his shop so I can't see how he could have."

Dumal nodded his head.

"As I said, we're keeping our minds open. One thing we did find was a broken display cabinet. A shard of glass from this cut his aorta, which means he would have died quickly and with little pain. I hope you can take some comfort in that."

Marie nodded her head, her eyes still buried in the tissue.

"The cabinet seems to have been taken from his wall, but there's no sign of anything that may have been in it, which is a little confusing. If we took you to the shop now, would you recognise this piece so we know what we're looking for."

"I really can't help you there, I'm afraid. I avoid the shop as much as possible. I hate to see those beautiful creatures pinned into showcases."

"I can understand that," said Dumal, who was already more interested in Marie than in finding out the truth about her husband's death.

"May I ask you some questions, or would you rather I came back another time once you've processed this?" he asked in a further pretence of sympathy.

Marie paused, wiping her eyes with a new tissue the detective had offered her seeing the first was now sodden.

"This is a huge shock inspector, but as you're here now please come in. I don't know how I can help, but I'll answer your questions as best I can. I last saw Xavier this morning at breakfast before he left for work. Or rather I heard him as we rarely breakfast together. He leaves so early."

She burst into tears again.

"I didn't even get to say goodbye to him."

"It won't take long, I promise."

"Would you like tea or coffee, or something stronger?" Marie asked him, dabbing her eyes to stem the flow of her tears.

"I can't drink on duty, madame, but if you don't mind I'll make a coffee for myself. I realise this must be extremely upsetting for you and a lot to take in. So please sit down and try to calm yourself. Can I get you anything?"

Marie shook her head and told him where he could find the kitchen. Dumal entered it and saw some coffee that looked recently brewed.

He poured some and took a sip. It was lukewarm but that would have to do as he had never learnt how to use the polished metal, high end coffee machine the Deschamps had installed. One day I'll have all this and more, he thought to himself, jealous to be in a home far more opulent than his own.

With his cup in hand he walked to the large, equally impressive American style refrigerator to get some milk as the coffee was far too bitter for his taste. He hadn't eaten all day so he also broke off a piece of what remained of a large cake on an exquisite kitchen island, fashioned from a flawless piece of marble. Quickly swallowing the cake and licking his fingers, he returned to Marie.

She was sitting on a beautifully patterned divan that perfectly matched the other furniture, in her home. Dumal could feel the thickness of the carpet beneath his feet. Everything from ceiling to floor screamed high end materials put together meticulously by an expert interior designer.

But Marie was by far the most beautiful thing in the house. Her lilac pencil skirt perfectly outlined the slenderness of her legs and her crisp white blouse, with the top two buttons unfastened, gave enough of a hint of her cleavage to make made him yearn to see more. So much more.

Taking out his notebook, he started.

"So, you are Marie Deschamps?"

"Yes"

"And your age?"

"35"

"Really? You look a lot younger."

"You're very kind"

"Children?"

"No"

Even better, thought Dumal.

"You look somewhat familiar to me, Madame Deschamps. Have we met before?"

"We haven't, Brigadier, but I am, or rather was, an actress. You may have seen me in a few ads, theatre plays or programmes on TV."

"I can see why you've been on TV" said Dumal, looking at her up and down in a way that made Marie feel uncomfortable. He moved towards her divan and gestured to ask if he could sit down beside her as he needed the side table to place his coffee.

"So tell me about your husband. Xavier, correct?"

"Yes, Xavier. There's not a lot to say really. He ran a shop selling insects to collectors. It was his life. I was a bit of an accessory, only brought out on special occasions to impress his friends because I was a very minor TV celebrity."

"Not to say a very attractive one, Marie."

"Thank you again, inspector," said Marie who was feeling more uncomfortable by the minute as she felt Dumal edging nearer to her on the divan. "But can we continue with the questions please?"

"Of course, I'm sorry. I meant nothing by it. How was the state of your marriage?"

"Fine. We hardly saw each other to be honest. He was tied up in his shop and his travels to find the rarest, most collectible insects. In return he gave me a generous allowance to do what I wanted. He didn't want me working any more, especially acting. He was a very jealous man, and was convinced some handsome actor would sweep me off my feet and steal me away from him."

"Understandable. And, if you'll forgive me for asking, has there been anyone?"

Marie blanched.

"No. I would never do anything to hurt Xavier like that."

Dumal looked around the beautifully furnished apartment.

"Your husband was clearly very wealthy."

"His wealth was more to do with a very large inheritance he received when both his parents died in a car crash when he was 17. He was an only child so received everything, including this home. It was their money that allowed him to pursue his odd passion for selling dead insects. The shop only makes a small profit, but he doesn't care. And he doesn't need to financially. So here I am in this palace of his, mostly alone all day."

How perfect for me, Dumal was thinking to himself. But he had to continue to feign his compassion and professionalism.

"Was your husband acting strangely, or feeling depressed lately"

"Not at all, but as I said, we were rarely together."

"So it was unlikely he'd take his own life?"

"Very unlikely. That shop was he life and he loved it."

"And did he have life insurance?"

"Yes I believe so. He told me when we married that had arranged a policy substantial enough to make sure I'd be comfortable for the rest of my life."

"When you say 'substantial', how much are we talking about?"

"I think around 10 million francs, but it could be

more. I really don't know and he never told me."

Dumal wrote this down in his notebook already imagining that house by the sea.

"So with this apartment and his other assets, you're set to be very comfortably off."

"Well, yes, I guess so. But that's not something I want to think about right now. I'm not a suspect am I?"

"Of course not. I do have to ask though…"

"What's that, Brigadier?"

"What were you doing tonight, from around 5pm to 7pm. We believe that's when your husband's death occurred."

Marie breathed a sigh of relief.

"I had friends around for coffee and cake and a bit of a gossip. It's something we do every weekend. Today it was my turn. You've just missed them actually, but I can give you their names if you need to check. Plus as you've just seen the coffee is still warm and there's what's left of the cake in the kitchen.

"And they were the only people in the house?"

"Yes. Well, actually no. Philippe was here too, a photographer friend of mine. He was taking pictures of my street as part of a new project of his on the architecture of the city. I invited him in to join us and warm himself up as it was getting cold outside. He's such a perfectionist he won't stop until he's certain he has the perfect shot. I'm sure all my friends will back up my alibi."

"Marie, er, I mean Madame Deschamps, please don't worry yourself. I absolutely believe but what you're saying, but as you'll understand I must follow police procedure. I have to ask these questions to eliminate you from our enquiries. But to tick all the boxes, I will need the contact details of your guests this evening."

Then he added, smiling as warmly as he could manage, "And don't worry, you seem nothing like a killer to me. And I've seen plenty."

Marie went to a writing table and opened her address book. She wrote down the names and addresses of her friends that afternoon on a piece of paper and passed it to Dumal. He placed it in his notebook, rising from the divan and thanked Marie for her cooperation at such a stressful time.

It looked like he was then about to embrace her as a show of sympathy, so she gracefully stepped back, hoping he would realise this subtle snub would show him she was not interested in anything other than him finding out what had happened to her husband.

"Again, I'm very sorry for your loss Madame Deschamps. And as I said, I will keep you fully informed of our investigation."

Dumal, of course, had not noticed Marie's gesture of rejection as he never expected women to be anything but dazzled by him. He was thinking that the upcoming inquest into Marie's husband's death would give him plenty of time to get to know her better, and impress her with his stature in the force. It worked with most women, after all, whether they were married or single.

"Thank you Brigadier" said Marie, escorting him to the door, which she closed behind him with more than a little relief.

CHAPTER 13

The day after killing the shopkeeper, Alex scanned the papers for any news of his previous evening's act.

There was nothing.

He double checked, but it was just the usual political stories and commentaries about them. Then it was the business pages, more opinion pieces on subjects of no interest to him and then the sports results.

But nothing at all about a strange death in the centre of the city.

Perhaps, he thought, this was because the body hadn't been found until the morning, or the police were searching for clues as to whether it was a murder or a suicide.

He was sure there were no witnesses to the crime, and fortunately he had been wearing gloves as there was still a chill in the air at dusk. He knew the most fashionable shops had CCTV installed but not that row of ancient shops. So even the most sceptical detective would have very little to help him investigate any suspicion of a criminal hand in the matter.

The most likely decision for the police, therefore, was to view it as an accident or a suicide, however strange the method used seemed.

This proved to be correct, because the next day the papers had got hold of the incident.

They reported a strange death in an 'old entomology boutique' that the authorities were treating as an accident or suicide. They said the enquiry was ongoing due to a possibly missing item from the shop. They were appealing for witnesses or for anyone who had bought anything from the shop that day.

It was only then Alex realised he had taken the beetle with him in the daze he was feeling at the time. Quite why he'd done this, he didn't know. But maybe, deep in his mind, he wanted to free such a beautiful creature, even in death, from that hideous mortuary in which it had been preserved for who knows how long.

But now the beetle had to disappear for good.

CHAPTER 14

Alex was living at that time in the Cité Universitaire, just south of the Parc Monsouris near the inner traffic ring of the city.

This is a place where around 6,000 students from around the world live at affordable rates so they can study in Paris. Over 25 different countries have buildings there, typically built in the traditional style of their homeland. These are all located in a large park, with separate cafeteria and theatre buildings too. It was and remains a beautiful place to explore.

The Résidence Franco-Britannique is a red brick building of six floors near the front of the park. It was here that Alex's university had placed him for his year of work and study in Paris. Several times a week he would jog around the whole park taking in the different styles of architecture from countries as diverse as Sweden, Nigeria and Peru. Thanks to this he knew exactly where to hide the beetle.

This was in a dense copse of bushes at the far south western extremity of the park, where his fellow students never went and where no-one could see him from the windows of their rooms.

Alex had already chosen the beetle's coffin. It was a white metallic biscuit tin that would be easy for Alex to bury deep in the moist soil. He made the deepest hole he could manage with a discarded and rusty trowel he had found in park, not wanting the tin to ever be found so human eyes could once more stare at what it contained.

The day after, the papers had more on the insect seller story. Labelling it a strange mystery, they described the unusual manner of Monsieur Deschamps' death, along with a theory that it may have been a robbery gone wrong, although there was still scant evidence to suggest this.

Alongside the story was a picture of what they had labelled his grief-stricken wife, only she didn't appear to be overly mourning the passing of her husband. In fact in her face Alex saw a flicker of relief that intrigued him. He also felt that intense attraction that sexually inexperienced men of his age often feel for such attractive, if more mature women.

In fact she was one of the most beautiful women Alex had ever seen. Even in the grainy black and white picture in the newspaper she radiated an intoxicating sense of gentleness and warmth.

He determined he would somehow meet her, not to confess to the seemingly senseless murder of her husband, but to get to know her better and discover whether, as his instincts were telling him, the effects of his actions hadn't traumatised her deeply.

Her name was Marie Deschamps, the paper reported. She was apparently an actress who lived with her husband Xavier in the upmarket Monceau region of Paris, far from the scene of the crime. The article made it clear she wasn't a suspect in the investigation, which was being handled by one of Paris' most senior detectives.

Alex had her name now, but how was he supposed to find her?

If this was a movie, he thought to himself, he'd go to his victim's burial, watching from a distance as a coffin was slowly lowered into the ground. The poor wife, with a black veil quietly sobbing over the grave.

But he also knew from these films that any suspicious police inspector might be there too, looking for unknown onlookers to question. He wasn't prepared to take that risk.

A Brigadier was indeed standing beside Marie in the photograph, but there was a strange body language between them. If looked like Marie was trying to turn her body away from him. Little did Alex know that this Brigadier was nothing like he seemed, for all the finery of his uniform.

Alex stared at the photograph, driven by an overwhelming desire to find this woman. But how?

As it turned out, they found each other.

CHAPTER 15

Brutus had quit his job as soon as he had tracked down Dumal. And as Paris even then was one of the most congested cities in Europe, he bought himself a scooter so he could more easily follow his prey to its lair.

He had to fight the temptation to strike immediately. He would be too obvious a suspect if Dumal was killed within a few weeks of his release from La Santé. Brutus would rather die than return there, especially as if he was caught it would mean the rest of his life spent in a concrete cage.

What he could do, however, was take a good look around Dumal's apartment so he could work out how best to abduct him when the time was right.

A few days later, when he had seen Dumal leave his apartment for work, Brutus put his plan into action.

The Brigadier's home was in a quiet street called the Rue de la Verrerie. It was typical of the traditional Parisian apartment blocks that gave the architecture of the city such cohesion. A large solid door gave access to all the apartments, with an array of buzzers with names beside them showing visitors which button to press to be allowed in.

Brutus parked his scooter on a parallel street then walked round to the entrance of the block. He knew he had to be careful as a black man in such a neighbourhood at any time of day would arouse suspicion.

Fortunately that day his luck was in.

Just as he approached the entrance a resident walked out of the building, leaving the heavy wooden door to shut slowly behind him. Keeping it open with his foot, he scanned the names beside the buzzers and found Dumal's. His apartment was on the first floor.

Perfect.

Brutus entered the inner hallway before turning left to climb up a spiralling flight of stairs. There he found the elegantly carved wooden door of Dumal's apartment.

Brutus took a small leather wallet pouch out of his pocket. Or at least that's what it looked like to the untrained eye. But Brutus was far from untrained. A man doesn't spend seven years in prison without learning some new tricks, and a friendly cellmate of his had taught him how to pick locks of practically every kind. Dumal's door, with a standard household lock, was one of the easiest of all to crack.

Taking a small steel wrench and an equally small corkscrew-shaped rod from the case, he quickly aligned the inner plugs of the lock with their pins. It took him less than 30 seconds to reach the driver pin, which he simply had to turn to unlock the door.

It opened with a small click, and Brutus entered a stylishly furnished hallway that served all the other rooms in the apartment.

Treading gently across the apartment in case nosy neighbours below or above heard him, Brutus opened each door in turn until he found the living room. He was delighted to see this gave out onto the street.

Clearly Dumal had spared no expense in decorating his home. The modernist sofas were of exquisite design and made of the finest white leather. From the ceiling hung an extraordinary antler horn chandelier. On a nearby shelf, large cut glass tumblers sat next to a matching decanter no doubt containing one of France's finest brandies.

Brutus looked at these with both admiration for their design and disgust at what Dumal must have done to have been able to afford them.

Looking outside, he calculated the perfect spot from where to shoot Dumal with a sniper rifle. It was from a closed down hairdressing boutique where the first floor also looked uninhabited. If so, he could set up a rifle there and make the clean shot he needed. This had to be highly accurate as he didn't want to kill Dumal instantly. That would be too easy. Too kind.

He wanted the detective to feel a lot more of the pain he himself had endured as a result of Dumal's lies.

To help his aim, he calculated the exact spot in Dumal's window the bullet would need to enter to hit Dumal just below his shoulder as he was pouring himself a drink. Brutus attached a small, white adhesive spot onto the window here to guide him when the time came.

As Brutus himself had discovered at the hands of Dumal himself, a bullet entering the body below the shoulder would incapacitate the victim to the degree that they would not be able to shoot back.

Then he checked there was no telephone in the room. It was essential he had time to cross the distance between his shooting spot and Dumal's apartment before the inspector could call in assistance if able to and then drag him away before the police arrived. If that wasn't possible, he wouldn't be able to execute the rest of his plan.

Execute being exactly the right word.

CHAPTER 16

A few weeks later, Alex was walking around the vast interior of The Louvre when he saw a party on a guided tour. And there, among the ten or so people in the group, was what appeared to be the shop owner's widow, now dressed in a brightly coloured summer dress.

She looked even more beautiful than he had imagined. Her blonde hair was cut into an immaculate bob, revealing a swanlike neck. She was above medium height, slender and her skin had the same healthy glow he had only ever seen before in professional athletes.

Alex wasn't alone in his admiration. He noticed that when couples passed her, all the men (and even some women) would furtively glance over at her. Those who weren't subtle enough were instantly and angrily chided by their partners. Marie didn't seem to notice this or, if she did, she was probably so used to it that it no longer caused any reaction from her.

Alex was simply dumbstruck. There was an indescribable radiance about her that completely beguiled him.

Most men, he figured, would assume she would be married to a rich man she would never leave for anyone less than a richer, more handsome one. And certainly not for a young student like him. But of course Alex knew she was recently widowed and seemingly not too remorseful about it. So, with his new found confidence he decided to at least try to speak to her. If he didn't he would always regret it.

As the tour stopped at Vermeer's The Lacemaker, Alex surreptitiously joined the group, standing right behind this woman who held an almost hypnotic grip on him.

Vermeer stands out among other great artists for his astonishing ability to portray the illuminating effect of sunlight. In The Lacemaker the light streams from the right of the painting, illuminating the face of a young girl meticulously sewing the lace thread of a dress.

As if by fate, light streamed from the right through one of The Louvre's huge windows onto Marie's face, illuminating her perfect features as she gazed in admiration at the painting.

Moving beside her, Alex couldn't help but say, "It's beautiful isn't it".

The widow turned her face to him, smiled, and simply said, "It's beyond beautiful."

"There's also a small Vermeer painting in The National Portrait Gallery in London", he replied. He deliberately made an attempt to speak French in a more English accent than he actually had by then, hoping this would be noticed by her.

"But this is far more captivating. I could look at it for hours. And at you too."

"Excuse me?, she said, blushing at such forwardness. But at the same time he could sense the compliment had pleased her. He just smiled, now finally with the self-confidence to look her directly in the eyes.

"You sound like you're English," she said, composing herself. "But I thought the English were more reserved."

Alex bent towards her and whispered, "Perhaps my French is not correct, but to me you are as beautiful as anything Vermeer could paint. And, as history has shown, when the British want something, we try very hard to get it."

"And is it me you are trying to conquer now?" she whispered back. "I have strong defences."

Alex laughed.

"All I want is to get to know you a little better. Perhaps once the tour is over?"

"But you're not even on this tour" she giggled.

"That's true. But I'm happy to wait."

She thought for a moment, then smiled.

"One coffee, but only because you're more interesting than this tour guide."

They waited for the group to move to the next painting, then slipped away to the Café Mollien.

It was a typical museum café, modern inside but noisy too given the stream of visitors both inside and out, the chinking of glasses and china inside, excited chatter outside where visitors debated the works they had seen and where they should go next.

The noise required us to bend towards each other so we could have a proper conversation. And with this came that certain intimacy rarely achieved within 20 minutes of meeting someone for the first time.

"I'm Alex" he said, extending his arm.

"And I'm Marie, but in France we don't shake hands. Instead we kiss." And she kissed him on both cheeks, the second kiss seemingly a lot closer to his mouth than the first.

"I'll certainly remember that for next time." he replied.

"So what is a young Englishman like you doing in Paris, Alex?"

"Studying," he replied. And, looking again into her eyes, continued "and taking in the many beautiful sites of this city."

"What's your favourite?" she replied, either unaware of his flirting or choosing to ignore it.

"I love everything about Paris. The architecture, the culture, the food, the history. I'm actually studying for a French degree. We spend a year in work placements in France. The students are scattered across the country but I was fortunate to be offered a placement in Paris."

"You certainly were, Alex. So are you enjoying your time here?"

"Very much. Especially today. I'm having coffee with its most charming woman."

"That's very kind and I'm flattered. But I'm also a lot older than you."

"A little, perhaps. But that's not something important to me. I feel I need to tell you something?"

"Go ahead."

"OK, but will you promise to look away from me as I say this, because it's embarrassing enough already..."

Marie seemed surprised but charmed by his strange request. The English really were as reserved as she had been told.

"OK." She turned 90 degrees toward the food counter, laughing. "Go ahead, Sir Alex of England."

He took a deep breath.

"Never in my life have I been as captivated by a woman on first sight as by you, Marie. And I have the feeling you're as beautiful inside too."

She turned back to him with a puzzled but happy smile on her face. It was Alex's turn to be blushing.

"But you hardly know me."

"No I don't. But somehow I don't think I need to. I've always been a good judge of character, if I say so myself. My father is a woodworker, and he always told me it's not just how good something looks on the surface that counts, it's how strong it is underneath. I see both beauty and strength in you, Marie."

"So you know a woman never gets tired of compliments."

"I'm sure you get a great many, and from people a lot more appealing than me," he said. "But I really wanted to talk to you. This doesn't come naturally to me, as I'm sure you can tell. But I just had to say it.

There was a silence, then Alex said, "I'm sorry if I've embarrassed you. I'll go now and leave you in peace. Good bye Marie, it's been wonderful meeting you."

Marie laughed and put her finger to his mouth. Her skin felt so perfect on his lips he had to force himself not to kiss them.

"Shh" she said. If I wasn't interested in you, I wouldn't be here with you. And you haven't embarrassed me at all. I'm meant to be in mourning for my husband but he died a few weeks ago. You're the first person who has made me laugh since.

There was, again, no hint of sorrow in her face, voice or body posture that suggested any kind of deep sadness at her husband's death.

"I'm so sorry" Alex replied. "Please accept my apologies for being so forward – and my condolences for the loss of your husband. I feel so stupid."

He took his coat, stood up and made to leave, hoping against hope she'd say something.

"Where are you going Alex? You may be a student, but clearly not of women. I can see you were being sincere about that. And sincerity is what I admire, as so many of the men in this city will say whatever it takes to get a woman into bed. But if you give up this easily you'll never get anywhere with any of us."

His heart leapt.

CHAPTER 17

Alex sat back down again, smiling as charmingly as he could muster. "Teach me then, Marie."

"OK, lesson one is that things aren't always as they seem."

She laughed as Alex made a pretence of writing notes on the café table.

"My husband was a decent man," she continued, "but not a husband in the usual sense of the word. He wanted me only as a trophy wife. We had no proper relationship to speak of, and I don't miss him. His only true love was for his insects."

"Insects? Did he breed them?"

"Ha, no. He sold them in his horrible little shop near Notre Dame. When he wasn't there, he was out looking for new specimens to sell. He would travel the world looking for them, leaving me at home to do as I pleased. It was an arrangement we had made before our marriage and it suited us both well."

"What was his name?"

"Xavier. He was wealthy. His house – now my house I suppose - is beautiful. Xavier was hardly ever there to enjoy it though. He had some very good qualities though, like doing all he could to boost my acting career. Unfortunately this isn't going so well. That's why I fill my days with tours like this, and with boring lunches with other 'ladies of leisure' as I believe you call them.

"I also have to endure the inquest into his death," playing the part of the grieving wife, whilst not feeling it at all. At least that's one area where my actress training will come in handy."

"So you're an actress! I want to work in the film world too once I graduate." As soon as he had said this, Alex immediately realised this might again make her think of the age difference between them, so he quickly changed the subject.

"What a strange relationship you and your husband had, but I guess every relationship is strange in different ways. And I'm sorry about your career. Why wouldn't a woman as beautiful as you make it in the film world?"

She blushed. "Now I know you're trying to seduce me."

Alex put his head in his hands.

"Oh God, I'm terrible at this. But I'm not very experienced at talking to women who affect me like you do. Especially in a foreign language. What can I say to make you like me?"

The gentle expression on her face sent a further frisson of desire through him.

"You're doing fine Alex, believe me. I'm very flattered and you make me laugh too. I also notice your French accent has improved dramatically in the last 15 minutes. You already speak excellent French."

"Are you trying to flatter me now? My French comes and goes, but it's generally at its best after a few glasses of wine. So have I flattered you enough to let me take you for dinner tonight or any night, for that matter? Fluent French, some more comedy, deliberately or otherwise and good food. What else could a sophisticated woman like you want?"

She thought about this for a minute, then nodded her head.

"That would be lovely she said. But as you're no doubt an impoverished student, and I'm a wealthy widow, I insist I pay."

"Really? You'll have dinner with me" Alex said, hardly believing what was happening. "You've just made me the happiest man in Paris. And I'm sure you'll know a restaurant far better than I could afford."

They set a time and place for that evening and kissed each other goodbye. This time even closer to the lips.

CHAPTER 18

Over dinner in the most expensive and lavish restaurant Alex had ever been to, Marie told him about herself.

She had always considered herself a Parisienne, having grown up in Fontainebleau, a satellite town of the city. It was most famed, she said, for its lavish palace that once held the Turkish Boudoir of Marie Antoinette.

Its large forest also attracted amateur and professional rock climbers from around France due to the large boulders scattered throughout it. She joked that if you took a walk through some of the paths, it was like being in a hallucinogenic dream with bright lycra clad figures visible all around you throughout the forest foliage.

She was the youngest daughter of two teachers, who had introduced her to literature, art and music, cultivating in her a love for culture that would never leave her.

From an early age she had dreamt of being a famous actress, dazzling the French public with her beauty and talent. Or otherwise she'd be a model, commanding the catwalks of Paris, Milan and London, being flown around the world, drinking champagne with other models and meeting the most handsome men on earth.

At school she had acted in many plays, often taking the leading female role where the rapturous applause from an audience of her friends, classmates and their parents (hers of course the most vociferous), made her believe she really might have the talent required to be a star.

She said her parents always boasted to others about their daughter's looks, especially after she had finished second in a beauty pageant they had entered her into without telling her.

She was furious with them, but also secretly proud to be seen as so attractive. Now she really started to imagine that she could make her childhood dreams come true.

So at 17 she had left for Paris, where a friend had a small apartment she said they could share while she tried to start her professional career. Sadly, she said, that second place in the pageant was a curse that seemed to follow her throughout her career.

Once in Paris, she found an agent easily enough, but she always seemed to just miss out on the parts she auditioned for.

She was constantly being told there was one other actress who they felt was just that little bit better suited for the part. She suspected this was because she always refused to submit to the sexual advances of casting directors, both male and female. Apparently everyone knew the most ambitious actresses would do anything for the roles they knew could launch their careers. But Marie absolutely refused to do this, wanting to secure roles through her talent alone.

It was the same story with the model agencies, who said that while she was beautiful, she wasn't quite beautiful enough for their clients. What they really meant, of course, was that she needed to starve herself to meet their ridiculous requirements. Again, this was something she refused to do.

After a year or so, with her hopes fading and her savings running out, she had finally landed an acting role in a new daytime TV soap opera. She was to play the alluring temptress to a married businessman, creating a torrid love triangle that the drama writers love to use to create endless storylines. Despite this, the writing was terrible. But even she was surprised when the show was cancelled after just 10 months.

However, she was at least now a minor celebrity, occasionally recognised on the street, if only by old women who watched a lot of daytime television. And she discovered that even a slightly recognisable face could lead to TV ads for beauty products, TV 'celebrity' quiz shows and other endorsements.

These were tedious but so lucrative that she could finally afford to move out of her friend's apartment into a place of her own, where she was able to repay some of her friend's great generosity with pizza nights, boozy dinners and sleepovers where's they'd stay up all night in their pyjamas watching the romantic comedies they adored.

But as whatever fame she had achieved waned (no doubt because her core audience were steadily dying), she had found the advertising work drying up too. She was still failing to land the prime acting parts she yearned for too, forcing her to make a living acting in smaller dramatic productions. And it was here that she had met Xavier.

He'd apparently been infatuated with her since her soap opera days, watching every episode on the small TV in his shop. When the show was cancelled he was the first fan to write to the TV station begging for it to continue. But to no avail.

Then one day he contacted her. She was playing Portia in a modest production of The Merchant of Venice in a small theatre in Montreuil. When she returned to her changing room after the performance she discovered a huge bouquet of red roses, along with a card that simply said, "In total admiration, Xavier", along with a phone number she didn't recognise.

Intrigued by this, but hoping this mysterious man might be a casting director, or a talent scout, or have friends who were, she waited a few days then called the number.

She was disappointed, if flattered, to discover that Xavier was her biggest fan. He had excitedly pronounced that in this play, which he had seen every performance of, her talent totally eclipsed the other cast members. On matinée days he would even close his shop early so as not to miss a minute of her performance.

Although this charmed her, what really got her attention was when he said that several well-known celebrities, including actors, actresses and film and casting directors would regularly visit his shop, looking for unusual exhibits to adorn their luxury apartments.

He said he had always recommended her to them, should a female part be available, because she was such a versatile and brilliant actress.

"You really should at least give her a screen test" he'd always say. But most of these people, who get requests such as this almost every day, would make him vague promises they never kept.

Xavier had invited her to dinner so he could find out what parts she really wanted so he could better recommend her to his clients in the TV and movie world. He also took fifty of her agent's cards so they could contact her more easily when a part came up.

Marie explained to Alex that she was naturally nervous about this unknown but clearly sincere man. And if he was indeed telling the truth, this just might be her final chance of a real break into the higher echelons of the acting world. The fact he was so enamoured of her work also reasserted her belief in her talent which had been so gravely eroded by the sneering of certain critics at her acting in that one failed soap opera.

She decided she couldn't pass up the opportunity, so she agreed. And when Xavier took her for dinner to Le Fouquet's, one of the finest restaurants in Paris, she realised he must have considerable wealth and therefore hopefully the contacts this tends to attract.

Xavier, at that time, was indeed quite charming and the man she described seemed very much at odds with the ill-tempered, obese man that Alex had encountered in his shop.

Xavier and Marie had discussed many things about her career, with him seeming to know more about it than she could remember herself. When she admitted it was now going nowhere and she might have to return to Fontainebleau, he was horrified.

He insisted she came to stay with her. He explained he had a large home with three unused bedrooms and that she could stay as long as she wanted, rent-free, to pursue her acting. He said she couldn't waste her talent and beauty doing some menial job back in the suburbs.

Maybe it was the wine that had been freely flowing all night, or her desire to make one last attempt to make a star of herself that made Marie agree to see his home then decide. It was indeed opulent and Xavier insisted he had no ulterior motives other to play a small part in her inevitable success. So Marie agreed.

As time progressed, of course, Xavier confessed little by little how bewitched he was with her beauty and always had been. And that if she were to marry him, she'd make him the happiest man in Paris. A nobody like him, married to Marie Lavigne, the celebrated actress and national treasure he was convinced she'd become.

He promised there wouldn't be a sexual element to the relationship. He had no sex drive as such, as every fibre in his being was obsessed with finding, capturing and collecting insects. Indeed, she could even have affairs if she was discrete about them so as not to embarrass him with the few friends he had. He also said he would rarely be at home anyhow as his work took him all over the world.

It was the strangest proposition Marie had ever heard, but as his opulent home in such a prestigious part of the city was sure to impress casting directors, and his terms of their relationship so loose, she had accepted. She had already got tired of other suitors who would all use the same chat-up lines in pathetic attempts to seduce her, sleep with her, then move on to the next woman.

Xavier and Marie married after just a few months and she had found herself with the same freedom as before but now with a home befitting an actress of the stature she needed to portray.

To Alex's surprise, Marie insisted that Xavier had been true to his word too. He had never made any sexual advances to her, growing increasingly distant as his passion for entomology completely consumed him.

Then he had died and Alex had entered her life.

CHAPTER 19

As Brutus was leaving Dumal's apartment, he heard from below the sound of a key opening the building's front door.

A figure entered, muttering to himself in a voice that Brutus remembered all to clearly. The voice that had spewed lies hour after hour in court to ensure his conviction. A voice that showed no remorse for the life he was ruining. A voice Brutus would cut from him as soon as he had the brigadier at his mercy.

Dumal must have forgotten something and returned for it. Five minutes earlier and he would have caught Brutus in his home, unarmed. He clicked the door shut as quietly as possible, but the sound still echoed down the staircase.

Brutus knew Dumal must have heard this. Now he had two choices. One was to run further up the staircase, but this would almost certainly make Dumal suspicious there was an intruder in the building. So he chose the second option, descending the staircase as confidently as he could, even nodding a greeting to Dumal as the two men passed.

As he did, Brutus noticed a flicker of recognition on Dumal's face. But it was just a flicker and Brutus was certain Dumal hadn't recognised him. He was, after all, one of many immigrants that

Dumal had no doubt jailed over the years to afford the apartment he had just left.

As for Dumal, he pondered for a second why Brutus' face seemed familiar to him, then shrugged and unlocked his apartment door. Black faces all looked the same to him, after all.

As he went to pour himself a large brandy, he noticed a tiny white sticker on the inside of his window. He peeled it off, wondering where on earth it could possibly have come from.

He screwed it into a tiny ball with his fingers, flicked it into a bin then slumped onto a sofa. All he really wanted to think about right now was Marie.

CHAPTER 20

At the age Alex was then, it was difficult for him to understand what love really was.

In his mid-teens he'd had transient infatuations, as is normal. They would end as swiftly as they arrived, as he was too tongue-tied to even try to talk to the girls who appealed the most to him.

His mother would despair at never seeing him bring a girl home, always telling him how handsome he was and that girls were always looking at him. But he ignored her words. Mothers always said such things to their sons, whether they believed it or not. And no girls had ever approached him other than to ask about other friends of his that their friends wanted to be introduced to.

But with Marie it was so completely different.

They were two people who had the strongest of bonds from the first time they met. The age difference meant nothing to either of them, and neither cared what other people thought anyhow. They were living a wonderful life together, not thinking of the future and Alex's return to England.

Every walk along the Seine, every candlelit dinner and every film they watched together in the darkness, hands caressing or gripping each other, brought them closer. Every kiss radiated the warmth inside them that they both craved. Every day, as Alex worked or studied, his mind would drift to her and how happy she made him feel.

He could never bring himself to tell her that he was the person who had killed her husband. They were both so much happier now and he couldn't bear the thought of that happiness ending because of an act he had never planned and a death he had never intended.

The investigation into Xavier Deschamps' death was quickly terminated.. No-one had come forward to say they had purchased anything, and the tag attached to the mahogany case found beside Xavier's body suggested he had indeed sold whatever was in it just before his unfortunate accident. After a mercifully short inquest, a verdict of death by misadventure was recorded.

Alex was in the clear.

Marie and he never spoke about Xavier, but every time she moaned while they made love or bit his arm as she orgasmed, any pangs of guilt he felt about killing him dissipated further. She was a loving, beautiful and cultured woman who had been denied true love for too long. He was delighted to be giving her real happiness after the marriage of convenience he had put such an abrupt end to.

This was indeed real love and Alex couldn't bear the thought of ever losing Marie. So he decided to stay in Paris with her, abandon his degree and become a private English tutor. He knew his parents would be furious as they had always expected him to pursue what they regarded as a proper career. For them, success was a job in insurance, accountancy or banking. These were professions that Alex had never wanted and would never have endured.

There was no way he could have made them think differently, or explain his love of a woman 16 years older than himself, so he never even tried.

Marie responded to his news with a shriek of glee and insisted they went to the Louvre to see the Vermeer painting where they had first met, then dinner at the restaurant they had gone to on their first date.

They would end the evening watching the famous cabaret show at the Moulin Rouge, which would, she joked, cement Alex as an honorary Parisian. Then, as cliché demanded, they would make love in front of the log fire at Marie's before waking together, their naked bodies pressed together as the last embers of the fire died down.

CHAPTER 21

Alex was quickly able to find work as a language teacher and a translator, the latter of which was paid by the word, and so was especially lucrative. He was paid in cash so he could remain outside the complicated French taxation system, at least until he had acquired a formal work permit.

He and Marie hardly needed the money, but Alex wanted to show how committed to their relationship he was. They decided the money he earned would be saved and pay for the many trips they had planned to see the world together.

They would often discuss these, curled up together on the sofa in Marie's living room. Their only disagreement doing this was choosing the order in which they would visit them.

Most of Alex's pupils were ambitious business people who needed proficiency in English to move up the corporate ladder. And as they could only take lessons at night, this left Alex free to discover the city at his leisure during the day.

It also meant Alex got to see many different parts of the city he would never otherwise have ventured to, little knowing how important this knowledge would soon prove to be. Having more free time during the day than in a normal job was a liberating experience and confirmed he was right in his decision to abandon his academic studies to be with the woman he loved so deeply.

His favourite client was one of Marie's best friends, Thérèse. He gave her English lessons for free because of this, despite her insistence she could and should pay. She put as much diligence into her language learning as her work as a lawyer and quickly became an excellent English speaker and a close friend of Alex's too.

One evening, as a test of how good her English had become, he asked her to explain how France worked as a country.

She frowned, let out a sigh and shrugged her soldiers.

"This is difficult. Because we have big problems. Corruption is everywhere, from politics, to police, to industry. Bribes and favours among the elite have been so frequent for so long, they are basically accepted by the people as intrinsic to French life. Nothing is ever done about it.

"You must realise, Alex, that if you are not part of the right people, you don't count at all in this country. So if you want to make it to the, how do you say, top table, you need to tread on many others to get there. This is why I work hard to be a lawyer. I want to prosecute these people who will ruin the lives of others to improve theirs. But the higher they get the more untouchable they become. And being a woman makes it even harder for me to be trusted to face these people in a courtroom."

Looking at her speak so passionately he could see why she was one of Marie's best friends. She wanted to help create a fairer society, however stacked the odds were against her.

"That's perfect English, Thérèse. And sadly it's the same in England and has been for centuries. Those who have power control those who don't, legally and illegally. The closer you get to exposing their crimes, the more they attack you. You're called a radical, an idealist or a dreamer, as if these qualities are a slur. If you demonstrate huge social inequalities, you're labelled as an agitator or a communist. So everything goes on as it always has, with the rich getting richer and even more powerful, and the poor getting poorer and even more exploited, as if this is the natural way of the world."

Thérèse nodded throughout Alex's increasingly angry rant. They shared the same opinions of the world's injustices, only Thérèse was doing everything she could to fight them.

Neither of them knew it yet, but this was just as well given what was about to happen.

CHAPTER 22

One evening, Alex returned from a lesson in La Defence, the French business area, where he had been teaching a group of Japanese bankers.

He entered the living room to find Marie looking pale and scared. He immediately kneeled down beside her and held her hand.

"What's wrong darling?"

As tears welled in her eyes, she told him a police inspector by the name of Dumal, who had investigated her husband's death, had called in yet again on a pretext about it. She explained that he had made several such visits over the last weeks, even though the inquest was over and the case closed. Each time he visited, he'd make it a little clearer that he wanted to see her now she was a widow. The thought of this disgusted her.

"He's increasingly touchy feely with me and just won't take a hint when I say no to his advances. I've told him I have a boyfriend but he doesn't seem to care."

"Why didn't you tell me about this before?" Alex said in astonishment.

"Because I thought he'd eventually give up. But he just won't. And today he told me I should leave you and date him. When I refused, he said he could make our lives very difficult. He didn't specify how but I assume he means lots of police harassment.

"He doesn't know you're English yet, but if he finds out he could prevent you from ever getting a work visa to live here. If you're found guilty of any crime, you'd never be allowed one either. And I have no doubt he's the kind of man who would fake something to ensure that too."

Alex was stunned.

"Who the hell does this guy think he is? Can't we make a complaint and insist he stays away from us in the future. Then, if he tries to do anything against me, at least we'd have the complaint on record."

"That's not the half of it," said Marie, seemingly scared to tell Alex any more.

"Tell me please, darling."

"When I refused him again, he became angry, as if he wasn't used to people saying no to him. He told me I must have been a terrible wife to Xavier if he preferred spending his life in a shop instead of with me. I asked him to leave immediately, thanking him again for his work on the case but saying as this was now closed there was no reason for him to call in again. He went silent and got up to leave. But as I was about to open the door for him, he lunged at me, trying to kiss me and God only knows what else.

"What? I can't believe this? How did you stop him?"

"Fortunately I was able to knee him, well, down there, and he fell back onto the hallway radiator, tearing his jacket."

"His jacket? Wasn't he wearing a police uniform?"

"Ah, that's another thing. He came in civilian clothes, so clearly he wasn't here on official business. Alex, I just don't know what I can do to get rid of him."

"Do you think he might have tried to…?"

Marie started sobbing again.

"I don't want to think about that, but yes, I wouldn't put it past him. I saw something so dark in him that I never want to see again."

Alex hugged her, stroking her hair.

"My poor darling. How did you get rid of him?"

"The fall seemed to have hurt his arm – the elbow of his jacket being torn. He stood up, glared at me and the look in his eyes was one of pure malice. Then he left, slamming the door so hard I thought it would break. It was horrible."

At that moment the doorbell rang. Alex opened it to see a man smiling a little sheepishly, though he could tell at once this was feigned. He seemed surprised at my presence, if not a little irritated.

"César Dumal," he announced himself. "Of the Paris Police. May I speak with Madame Deschamps please?"

"Dumal..." Alex replied, staring him straight in the eye. "We've just been talking about your behaviour today. I assume you've come back here to collect the part of your jacket you left behind".

"And who are you?"

"I'm Alex Amis, Marie's friend. Normally I'd shake your hand, but I don't like attempted rapists and we don't want you in this house ever again. All we need from you is the name of your superior. Your actions today go way beyond serious misconduct and you should be fired from the force."

Rather than respond, Dumal shouldered Alex aside and entered the living room where Marie sat, frozen in her chair with fear.

"Why do you keep hounding me, Brigadier! Have you no shame after what you did today?"

Calmly Dumal took the seat opposite her. "I am here to apologise. What I did and said earlier was wrong, but I felt during the investigation of your husband's death that there was a spark between us. I acted impulsively this afternoon and I shouldn't have. Please accept my sincerest apology."

Marie raised her fearful eyes to his and said, as calmly as she could, "I will ask you again, Brigadier Dumal. Please leave me alone to mourn my husband's death. We both know what you did and what your intentions were. Reporting you seems to be the only way to put an end to this kind of behaviour and get you out of my life. How people like you can get to positions of such power in the police force is beyond me. You're little more than a jumped-up thug who thinks he can take what he wants."

Dumal put his hands together, as if in prayer, Alex noticed a tattoo on his right wrist. It was of a laurel leaf crown, with a single word inscribed on it. 'Caesar'. This man really did think he was some kind of all-powerful emperor.

"I'm sorry you feel this way, Marie. And that we got our signals crossed. But let's consider any allegation you make against me," began Dumal.

"It would be your word against mine. Me a senior police officer with an unblemished record, you a recently widowed woman prone to all kinds of emotions. No evidence of any kind of attempted rape, as you so charmingly put it, and no motive. What do you really think you'll achieve?"

"You truly are a despicable man. You can't even see the damage your actions cause. Everything is about you and what you want. And when you can't have it, you act like a spoiled child. If you have a wife, which I sincerely doubt, I'd be truly scared for her safety."

Dumal's eyes hardened at the mention of his ex-wife, and Alex could see the same enraged look Marie had described to him just minutes before.

Dumal had to struggle not to stand up and punch Marie. That frigid bitch of a woman he'd married was just the same. And she had dared to accuse him too.

"I think you'd better leave now *César*," Alex said firmly, pronouncing his name ironically to show how pathetic he found it. "You'll know very soon about our complaint."

Dumal looked up at him disdainfully, shaking his head.

"English I assume," he snorted. "The nation of shopkeepers. I suggest you go home before you find yourself butchered."

"I think you're confusing Napoleon with your obvious hero, César. And it's you that's going to be in trouble. And it's you that's going home too. Right now."

Dumal, never one to back down, bent towards Marie and whispered, "Make a complaint about me and you might find yourself reunited with your husband sooner than you expected."

Then he turned and made for the door, again elbowing Alex out of the way as he left.

CHAPTER 23

Dumal left Marie's house seething with rage.

How dare they threaten him, César Dumal. And who on earth was the man that told him to leave? He'd never set eyes on him before. Perhaps he was a relative, but no, that couldn't be right. He was English and there was a sense of intimacy about the two that suggested a close relationship. Marie was rich and beautiful, yes, but such a substantial age gap must surely preclude anything like that.

And if it was amorous, so soon after her husband's death, then maybe this was a murder after all. A murder she'd had that man carry out to inherit his fortune.

Maybe he could imprison the Englishman for it, perhaps, whether or not he had any involvement in it. But would it be worth the effort for a woman even he had to accept would never now be interested in him.

Dumal could hardly go back and question the man tonight, but could of course interrogate him on his own turf, if he could fabricate a motive to do so.

That, though, would be for another day. Tonight he needed to assuage his fury and he knew exactly where to do it. The Rue Saint Denis.

CHAPTER 24

The Rue St. Denis is one of Paris' oldest streets. It is also one of its most dangerous. But Dumal was happy when he arrived to see it packed with addicts buying various drugs and red-faced men talking to prostitutes. Takings must be good.

He hated the people he collected money from. They preyed on the weak, the lonely and on the waifs and strays of the city. He never understood the irony that he was just like them. And if he had, he would have rejected this instantly. What they did was so evidently sordid, whereas he was a protector of the good, especially when it was for his own benefit.

When he broke the law it was in ways people never saw. And, he felt, for better reasons too, not least to give him the lifestyle he deserved.

Those he hated most of all were the ones who didn't pay him his due. The ones who scorned his power. Did they think they could dismiss him as a nobody when he could arrest and charge them all if the fancy took him.

He had a speech ready whenever people couldn't pay him.

"What would you do if a punter didn't pay you for sex, or for a bag of cocaine? You'd get angry. You'd get violent. You'd hurt them. I do the same. And if you still don't pay, I have to take things further. So you choose."

He knew they couldn't afford to ignore him. If he put them in hospital for just a few days they'd have been replaced with new whores, pimps or drug dealers. But he'd then have to explain to all of them again the weekly payments expected if they wanted to be left alone to ply their filthy trade - and of course the consequences of non-payment.

When Dumal had taken control of the street, he knew he was entering dangerous territory. The French Mafia would always be watching him, and would kill him in a heartbeat if he played his hand badly. He also knew that the key to extortion was looking in total control of his operation. And he was determined to look particularly strong that night, taking out his anger on whoever gave him an excuse to do so.

He made straight for the street corner where the indebted drug pusher was always working. It didn't take long to find him, counting out a bundle of money with a smile on his face. That smile turned to fear as he saw Dumal approach.

"That must be for me?" he said smiling. "Only it doesn't look like the 10,000 you owe me. But I'm sure you've got the rest hidden somewhere."

"Sir, you gave me a week", stammered the dealer. It's only been 6 days."

"That's a fair point, my smack-dealing friend. So let's work this out. One seventh of 10,000 francs is what...around 1,400 francs. And 1,400 multiplied by 6 is?"

Dumal pretended he was doing this less than complicated calculation in his head, when in actual fact he'd put on this performance many times before.

"Well, I make that around 8,400 francs. But you can double check if you want. No? So, 8,400 francs is what you'll give me now. We'll collect the rest during tomorrow's normal round. And congratulations, I never thought you'd get the money in time. Maybe we're not charging you enough."

The man cursed himself under his breath for flashing his money that night, never thinking Dumal would visit a day early, so reluctantly he handed over the money which the inspector put inside a Vuitton leather bag before adjusting the figures in his roster.

Dumal had half hoped the dealer wouldn't have anything like that much money ready, giving him an excuse to unleash the fury he still felt. This continued to burn inside him as he took his journey home. So instead he focused his anger on a plan to destroy the people who refused to bow to him.

Alex and Marie.

CHAPTER 25

"Are you Alex?"

This was the first question the policeman asked Alex after ringing Marie's doorbell at barely 8am the next morning. He was accompanied by another policeman. Alex assumed this was to make their visit look legitimate and to intimidate him.

Alex nodded, yawning. "What's this all about?"

"Please come with us down to the station," one of them said.

"What? Why?"

"You'll find out when you're there, sir" said the other.

"What exactly is this? Have I done something wrong?"

He wasn't being arrested, they insisted, but they wanted to ask him a few questions about a case they were taking a fresh look at.

"What case?"

"We cannot tell you that I'm afraid"

Alex felt no panic. There really was no evidence linking the crime to him. And he was sure that no-one had seen him. The inquest should have put a definitive end to the affair. So he realised this was, indeed, Dumal demonstrating his power to make his life hell.

Marie came downstairs fastening her bathrobe. In the background you could hear the shower running and he would have far rather joined her there than spend what was sure to be another angry and frustrating encounter with that clown Dumal.

Seeing the officers standing beside Alex, Marie asked what was happening.

"I'm pretty sure it's Dumal playing games" he said. "They say they want to ask me some questions at the station. They won't even say what about, because they know it's one of his little amusements."

Then looking at the officers he said, "Did Brigadier Dumal send you here?"

The two gendarmes glanced at each other, shifting their feet uncomfortably. They nodded. They knew they had no right to take him from Marie's home without explaining why, but their fear of Dumal was too great for them to do anything but obey his orders.

"OK, you get dressed and go with these two." Marie said. I'll call Thérèse immediately and ask her to go to the station as soon as possible to get you out of there. And if, as I suspect, such intimidation is contrary to police regulations, Tweedle Dum and Tweedle Dee here will have to answer for their actions in front of a police tribunal."

The gendarmes looked genuinely worried now. They realised their careers could be on the line all because of the petty jealousies of their superior. They knew he would have no qualms about saying he hadn't sent them there, should a complaint about this be made.

"There won't be any interrogation, Madame," said one.

"Inspector Dumal just has a few questions to ask Alex," said the other. "He told us to come here if we didn't find him at his student residence. We didn't, so here we are."

"A 'few questions' sounds like an interrogation to me." Marie said sternly. "And if this is what it turns out to be, we'll make sure you and Inspector Dumal pay dearly for it."

CHAPTER 26

They put Alex in a small, white room which contained a table, a voice recorder and 3 plastic chairs. There was also, of course, a one-way mirror behind which, Alex assumed, Dumal was grinning like the idiot he clearly was.

A few minutes later Dumal entered into the room. He slowly walked towards Alex, smiling as if he had caught his prey. His face had never seemed more weasel-like.

He eased himself into his chair, his eyes never leaving his latest plaything. He was going to make Alex pay dearly for his mockery of him the previous day.

Alex looked up to the ceiling, then lowered it until it was level with Dumal's. He shook his head contemptuously.

"Inspector Dumal. How lovely to see you again. And what a coincidence you've brought me here before we had the chance to make our complaint about you."

He turned to the mirror, hoping someone else would be watching. Then he pointed at Dumal and shouted, "This is the man who tried to rape my girlfriend yesterday. I hope you're proud of your boss!"

"There's no-one there Alex, this isn't a movie. And I don't know what you're talking about. There's never been any complaint against me. You're here because I want to ask you some questions about the death of Madame Deschamps' husband."

"You can't be serious? Are you really going to question me about a closed case where an inquest has already concluded it was death by misadventure? If so, it means your two little messenger boys have just lied to me, and in front of a witness too. Even you must know I had nothing to do with the death of Marie's husband, you vindictive, petty bastard."

"Are you insulting an officer of the law, Alex?. I could have you arrested for that."

"I didn't realise rape was legal in France, Mr officer of the law."

"Last warning."

Alex remembered what Marie had said about Dumal finding a reason to have his residential permit denied him. So he had to avoid taunting him further until he had Thérèse there too.

He looked at the tape recorder in the interview room. It hadn't been turned on.

"Brigadier Dumal, if you're going to question me

as a suspect in a murder case – and one that has already been decided was not a murder, I want every word of this interrogation to be recorded - and my lawyer to be present."

Dumal ignored this and, opening a notebook, continued.

"What is your name?"

Alex shook his head in disbelief. He really was going to do this.

"Alex Amis"

"Nationality?"

"The same as yesterday. British. You'll perhaps remember telling me to go back there then?"

"If you say so. What's your date of birth Mr Amis?"

"1st August 1969"

"And what is your relationship with Marie Deschamps?"

"That's none of your business."

"Isn't she a bit old for you?"

"Well, that's for us to decide. Why are you so concerned that we're together? Is it because she's turned you down so many times, and for an Englishman? I thought Marie made this absolutely clear yesterday inspector. Charming though you think you are, Marie finds you a disgusting creep who she wants to NEVER, EVER see again."

Dumal clenched his fists, as Alex continued, unable to control himself.

"You know, I actually feel some pity you, Dumal. You clearly can't see there's more to loving someone than their age. I guess sex is the only value women have to you?. Then again, you look like the type of man who, when a wife or girlfriend finds out how abusive you are, would be dumped immediately. Is that right inspector? Is that why you're now using your little bubble of power to infiltrate the lives of vulnerable women like Marie?"

Dumal said nothing, but his face turned red and that look of anger he and Marie had seen the day before flared up again.

"My personal life has nothing to do with this," he snarled.

"Yet mine has, it seems. And I'm so sorry if, as your face and clenched fists are to go by, I have touched a nerve with you. Do you have a wife or girlfriend? I'm sure my lawyer would like to talk her."

Dumal coughed, straightened his tie and continued.

"I'm asking the questions here Mr Amis. And I'm asking you to tell me what you were doing on the evening of Saturday 7th June from 4pm to 6pm."

Alex let out a sigh of frustration. This wasn't an area he wanted or expected Dumal to go into.

"How can you expect me to remember that? It was months ago. All I can say is that before meeting Marie I spent most Saturday evenings in my room at the Cité Universitaire, studying. I'm an overseas student here as part of my degree course. As I work here too, I spend my weekends catching up on a course I'm taking on Economic Translation. It's at Paris IX Dauphine University if you want to check. So I would assume I was studying on the evening in question."

"Do you have a work and a residential visa? If not, you're breaking the law."

"I very much doubt that César, if you don't mind me calling you by your first name. All the paperwork is sorted by my university. It's a long-standing exchange programme so I doubt there's anything illegal about me living and working here. But please feel free to check. All I'm given is an identity card in case I'm ever asked for it by cops like you. As you deemed it fit to bring me here so early this morning, before I had even dressed, it's back at Marie's, but please feel free to come and check it. Oh, no wait, you're not welcome there anymore are you? Not since you sexually assaulted her. Allegedly, of course. For now at least."

"Oh, we'll check" Dumal retorted, ignoring Alex's last comment. He knew full well he'd get nowhere trying to prove Alex was in Paris illegally.

Instead he continued.

"Actually I prefer you call me Brigadier Dumal, given the circumstances."

"The circumstances being what? That you're illegally interrogating me?

"No. The circumstances being that your alibi for that Saturday is that you were studying in your room?"

"Yes, César, if you really feel I need to provide an alibi."

"And you were alone?

"Yes, I was alone, studying in my room."

"So you could have killed Xavier Deschamps?"

"I guess I could have committed any crime that took place that night in Paris if that is your reasoning, César. Why not charge me all the robberies and attacks that must have taken place that night too?"

Alex was starting to worry that Dumal might, after all, have some evidence linking him to Xavier's death. So he was relieved when at that exact moment Thérèse entered the room.

"What on earth is going on here," she exclaimed incredulously. "You have absolutely no right to interrogate my client like this, as you well know. Another officer should be here for one thing, and I don't see one."

"And he hasn't read me my rights either. This is just one of his vindictive games."

"I'm just asking him some questions about the death of Marie's husband, for which it seems Alex here has no alibi."

"An interrogation he's refusing to record for a reason he's declined to explain".

"Marie has filled me in", said Thérèse. Then turning to Dumal she said, "I didn't believe you could possibly act so flagrantly outside the laws you've sworn to uphold. You've gone too far this time, thinking you can intimidate my client to stop us reporting your behaviour. We're going to do so right after this farce ends, which is now."

Dumal shrugged dismissively. "I'm a police inspector investigating a potential murder case. I simply want to know what Mr Amis was doing on the night of the death of the husband of Marie Deschamps. I have no obligation to record our conversation. Mr Amis hasn't been arrested and is free to go at any time."

"And we're going right now," said Thérèse. "Straight to your superior. The Deschamps case is closed. The inquest has finished. It concluded Xavier Deschamps' death was misadventure. And if you want to continue with this vendetta against Mr Amis you should probably know that he hadn't even met Marie until after her husband died."

This was not something Dumal had expected to hear.

"I didn't know that. How could I?" he stammered. "I just wanted to ask him a few questions as he already seems very much part of Madame Deschamps' life. Is it beyond reason to suspect that Mr Amis here might have killed Mrs Deschamps because he'd started an affair with her? For all we know she may have wanted her husband gone as she'd fallen for this... toy boy."

Thérèse snorted in derision. "I think you'd better stop talking inspector. You're clutching at straws, and you know it. Are you seriously suggesting Marie Deschamps would ask an English Exchange Student, fresh to Paris, to kill her husband so they could be together?"

"I'm just following a new line of enquiry."

"What new line?"

"I can't tell you that"

"Please, please put this 'new line of enquiry' before a magistrate. You'll be the laughing stock of all Paris. It's bullshit and you know it. This is pure intimidation because Alex here has what you can't have. He's here because you know we're about to report you for trying to rape the wife of a recently deceased man. You yourself investigated the death of her husband. And during the inquest did you ever once raise the possibility about a murderer being involved? If you did, I certainly don't recall it."

Dumal glowered at Thérèse.

"No."

"Exactly. So this is all a bit of a coincidence wouldn't you say? Questioning the boyfriend of a woman you tried to rape yesterday."

"Rape! What nonsense" exploded Dumal kicking his chair back. I did absolutely nothing to her outside my remit as an investigating officer."

"Apparently in plain clothes, she said, holding up some material from his jacket. You left this on Marie's radiator when she, let's say, refused your latest advances. I'm sure we can match it to your jacket if you try to deny it. Let's see what your superior says then about another attack on a woman. I believe you having previous history in such things."

"So I was right!" exclaimed Alex. "You are a woman beater. I just knew it."

Dumal sprang up, raising his fist as if to hit Thérèse.

Thérèse simply placed the torn material on his fist, making Dumal look all the more ridiculous.

"Easy now, inspector. You won't get away with another incident of beating a woman. Not when she's a lawyer in the process of making a formal complaint against you. Maybe we could summon your ex-wife as a witness."

"You think a scrap of material is some kind of proof of violence? I simply slipped in her hallway, falling back and tearing my jacket on the radiator. Maybe I should sue Marie for having such a slippery floor."

"Oh yes, I'm sure that happens all the time with someone as slimy as you," Alex snorted in derision. "Maybe you need some new Roman sandals, César."

"One more quip from you and I'll have you arrested for insulting a police officer" Dumal snarled at Alex.

"Oh, I don't think you will," said Thérèse. "Come on Alex, we're going."

She eased him away from Dumal who looked like he was about to explode.

"Unless you want to formally charge my client, Brigadier."

Dumal stayed seated and slowly shook his head. He had lost this battle, but the war was far from over.

"And your superior is…?"

"Brigadier Chief Elise Baron. She's presently on holiday. I'm sure you can arrange to see her next week."

"I assure you we will. And just to be clear, my client has nothing whatsoever to do with the death of Marie's husband. There is nothing that could possibly place my client at the scene and no evidence he even knew Xavier Deschamps – or, as you suggest, he was seeing Marie. So I suggest you stop this nonsense immediately. In fact, if you mention it ever again, we'll add harassment to our list of complaints. Goodbye inspector."

Once they'd left the interview room, Dumal smashed his fist down on the table. This wasn't what was supposed to happen. But the threat of a complaint to Elise didn't faze him. After all, she too owed him a big favour.

As Thérèse and Alex headed for the exit, the two officers who had escorted him from Marie's home to the police station approached them sheepishly.

"Please don't include our names if you make an official complaint" said one.

"We're only probational police officers," said the second. And this could end our careers before they've even started. We were only following Brigadier Dumal's orders. If cadets like us cross him in any way, he makes sure they are sacked for insubordination."

Thérèse looked at Alex questioningly.

"It's OK, I'm beginning to understand the nature

of your boss. You won't be included in our complaint."

Relief broke out on their faces and they thanked them before quickly leaving, clearly scared of Dumal catching them talking to the people who had humiliated him in his place of work.

"Thérèse and Alex looked at each other in astonishment, both wondering how Dumal could be allowed to control the Commissariat through such fear and intimidation.

"What on earth…?" Alex started.

"Don't worry, we'll find out soon enough."

CHAPTER 27

The next day, Brutus parked his scooter near the closed down hairdresser's shop. It looked like it hadn't been used for many months. All you could see were some dusty chairs left in front of dirty mirrors and an old comb on the floor. Dust had settled on the cans of hairspray that had been abandoned there. And to see these you had to peer through the few gaps that remained between the various flyers that had been attached to the dusty windows.

Brutus followed the narrow alley down one side of the building that led to the back of the shop. This was protected by a weather worn, flimsy wooden fence that Brutus didn't even need to kick to destroy. He simply pushed it over and found himself on a paved but derelict patch of land at the building's rear.

He could see a door. This was either the back entrance to the shop or, if he was lucky, led to the first floor, which he hoped was an uninhabited apartment not part of the shop.

Knowing he couldn't be seen from the front of the building, Brutus kicked open the door. It was indeed separate from the downstairs premises, with a flight of stairs leading straight up to the first floor.

Brutus climbed up to the stairs and opened the unlocked door that led to the empty apartment. Immediately he was hit by the overpowering smell of damp and decay. The floor was covered in old newspapers, and an array of spiderwebs that suggested it hadn't been lived in for months or even years.

He checked the rest of the apartment for any other stairs that might lead down to the shop below. There were none, so any potential renters of the disused hairdresser's would be oblivious to his presence above them as he prepared the next stage of his attack.

He moved to the front of the apartment and carefully parted the filthy curtains to see if he could see into Dumal's infinitely smarter apartment.

The view was perfect. He could fire a clean shot straight into Dumal's living room, then be there within just minutes to grab the stricken inspector and take him to what would be his final resting place.

He swore when he saw the white sticker was gone, but not worried. He could replace it any time, and he wouldn't need it anyway. He had such a perfect view into Dumal's living room that he was sure he couldn't miss him.

Brutus was far from an amateur marksman. He had been busy practising at a shooting range since his release and was a natural when it came to sniper rifles. With a good scope on one, he could hit a target up to 250 metres away. This shot was no more than eighty metres.

Everything seemed to be falling into place.

CHAPTER 28

As Thérèse drove Alex home from the police station, he wondered exactly what Dumal was up to. Was he really so petty as to bring him in to his station as revenge for being ejected from Marie's apartment so unceremoniously the day before? Or was it a warning to him of his power?

Whatever the case, it had backfired on the inspector. Alex now knew Dumal had no serious evidence linking him to the insect seller's death, but that he was desperate to convict him for something, simply to ruin his relationship with Marie.

He'd also been caught lying in front of a lawyer, and of interrogating him illegally, so how far was he prepared to go to do this?

Alex sensed his story about Elise Baron being on holiday was another lie. Dumal simply wanted more time to work out what to say to her when their allegations against him were presented in full.

He had to trust that Dumal's superiors would take immediate action against him. Otherwise he had no idea what Dumal might do next.

CHAPTER 29

Elise Baron was the very opposite of Dumal. She was the daughter of a Frenchman and an Indian mother. Her mother worked in a supermarket where she had met her husband, who was a warehouse manager.

Her parents never earned enough money to send her to the best schools, but had encouraged her to always work hard and do her best. If she did that, they said, she could never be ashamed of herself.

It was these principles that had seen her make her way to the top. She was dedicated to justice and her dedication and the long hours she put into her job were combined with an uncanny knack for understanding and tracking down killers that few other police could boast. Not that she had any chance of matching Dumal's conviction rate by staying within the law.

So Eloise was very surprised when she was appointed to the top post of Senior Brigadier of the Paris Police. Everyone, including her, had expected the role to go to César. What she didn't know was that he had turned down the job as it would mean too much hard work, work he knew would interfere with his more lucrative side activities. Needless to say he had couched this in very different terms.

He told the selection panel that Elise was a model policewoman, and that appointing her to the top role would be excellent PR for the force. Diversity was a hot topic in France at that time and this was the best way of showing the press and the country that talent and hard work paid dividends regardless of race or gender.

He almost laughed out loud when saying this, as he had always believed only men had the right qualities to be police and that 'half castes' as he called them had no place in protecting French citizens.

Unlike Dumal, Elise had only once exploited her position for her own means. And that once was when, several years previously, she had asked César to fix a complicated situation for her.

Her son had been caught dealing cocaine at the Sorbonne university. As a result, he faced both expulsion from one of the most prestigious universities in France and, even more terrifying for her, spending time in jail. This would prevent him following his mother into the Police Force, which he had planned to do.

After all the sacrifices her parents had made to help her succeed in life, she couldn't bear the thought of her doing nothing to save her son's career prospects.

When she confessed to Dumal her worries, Dumal promised to make the problem go away. He secretly removed the seized drugs from the evidence room. Then, declaring that only other officers whose duties involved guarding case evidence could have taken it, he had them all drug tested.

Sure enough, several were found to have traces of cocaine in their system, no doubt from weekend nights spent in the clubs of the city. Each officer was demoted in rank for breaking police rules. The case against Elise's son then collapsed through lack of evidence.

For Dumal this was the perfect result. The officers below him lived in fear of him, while his superior would protect him from any of his own discretions.

Eloise was immensely grateful at the time, but was about to discover it was the worst decision she would ever make.

CHAPTER 30

The minute they arrived back at Marie's apartment Thérèse called the police station and asked if would be possible to speak to Elise Baron. She was told Elise was currently busy, but to try to call back later.

So Dumal had indeed been lying. Again.

Shaking her head at this new proof of Dumal's behaviour, Thérèse added another complaint to an already long list. And when she called back later and asked for a meeting with Eloise to discuss the serious misconduct of Brigadier Dumal, Elise said she was shocked and yes of course Alex and Thérèse could see her. They set a time for 5pm the next day.

Together with Alex, she wrote up a formal list of complaints. When Thérèse had gone home, Alex went to join Marie in bed. He fell asleep immediately where he dreamt of being chased by Dumal across a heavily ploughed field, huge butterflies fluttering above them. He fell to the earth and there saw the huge beetle climbing and descending the tractor ruts. Atop it sat Dumal, dressed like a cowboy, his face grinning as he pointed a pistol at Alex's head. As he heard the sound of a shot, he woke up screaming.

He was soaked in sweat and staggered to the shower to cool himself down.

He had of course woken Marie, who joined him in the shower to comfort him. With her naked body gently pressed against his and her soft hands washing away the sweat from his neck and shoulders, he told her about the dream. She consoled him, saying it was just a nightmare caused by Dumal and that he would soon be out of their lives forever.

They went back to bed, where Marie kissed him lovingly, slowly caressing his arms until he fell into a deep, dream-free sleep until morning.

CHAPTER 31

Thérèse and Alex entered Eloise's office promptly at 5pm the next day. She was the very epitome of a senior policewoman, immaculately dressed with her hair tied back in a bun, her desk a shrine to neatness.

She asked them to sit down in the two seats that had clearly been arranged for them across from her desk. They thanked her for seeing them so promptly, to which she simply nodded.

"So how can I help you?"

Thérèse did most of the talking, explaining how Dumal had kept bothering Marie on the pretext of discussing her husband's death. This had quickly led from that to sexual overtures and then the incident at her home where he had physically assaulted her when she had refused his advances. She held up the material from Dumal's jacket as she explained how Marie had fought him off, and urged her to ask César to explain why he would visit her in civilian clothes to talk about a closed case.

She then explained how Dumal had treated Alex, once he knew he was with her. She asked why he felt he could have brought a foreign student into the station like a common criminal, interrogated him without a witness being present, refuse his requests for their conversation to be recorded and only relented when Thérèse had arrived as his solicitor.

She concluded by saying that Dumal had even suggested Alex might be responsible for the death of Marie's husband, despite the inquest's ruling and any evidence whatsoever.

Eloise listened intently, widening her eyes at some of the more serious actions they were describing, and nodding at the others.

When Thérèse had finished there was a long pause before Eloise spoke.

"These are very serious accusations that, if true, are clear grounds for dismissal and even prosecution" she said. "But we need physical proof."

"Marie wouldn't lie about being attacked," Alex exclaimed in frustration. "We have material from his jacket that shows he was in plain clothes when he claimed to be on police business. You can surely match that with his clothes that night. Do you not believe us?"

"it's not a question of whether or not I believe you, but whether you can prove what you're alleging."

Thérèse took over.

"The two officers who brought Alex here yesterday were clearly uncomfortable at basically kidnapping my client on his orders. When I entered the interrogation room I saw that Mr Amis was clearly being interrogated alone by Brigadier Dumal. He even lied about you being on holiday so we couldn't bring this complaint to you yesterday. I guess that was a ruse to give him enough time to fabricate his excuses."

"Please stop him! I'm scared for the safety of Marie and myself," Alex shouted, despite all his efforts to let Thérèse put forward their case.

"OK, Mister Amis. Please calm down. Shouting at me won't help anything," Eloise said calmy.

"I'm sorry, you're right. We're just at our wits end. We're not looking for Brigadier Dumal to be dismissed. We just want him to leave us alone. If he does, that will be the end of the matter. Surely that's the best result for everyone? But unless you intervene, we feel he will continue to harass Marie and Mr Amis, given his outrageous behaviour yesterday, whether or not you believe us."

"I understand your grievances and, as I have said already, it's not a question of whether or not I believe you. But as a lawyer, Thérèse, you must understand that I need more concrete evidence to take your accusations any further. Brigadier

Dumal is a highly respected member of my team and it is difficult to believe he would act this way. He has an unblemished record and I would need to see irrefutable proof that he has acted as you say before taking any action against him."

"But that's ridiculous," said Thérèse. The interrogation of my client yesterday was absolutely illegal. That on its own surely merits sanction?"

"As you should know Thérèse, there is a big difference between a conversation and an interrogation. Perhaps inspector Dumal went a little too far in his questioning of your client, for which I apologise, but you must understand that if he has unanswered questions about any case, closed or not, he is justified in asking them. As I understand it, your client was not put under arrest nor obliged to answer any of the Brigadier's questions."

"Something he never made my client aware of."

"Again, can you prove this?"

"Not when there are no witnesses in the room or any recording of the interrogation."

"Exactly. Which is why I'm afraid I can't help you with this at this point. The only physical proof you have is a shred of a jacket that could easily be explained away. I will of course follow up this matter with Brigadier Dumal, but I'm not going to take your word against his. Even if I did, I can assure you that a police tribunal would never find in your favour."

A silence descended in the office. Then Eloise asked them to leave as she had many other tasks to do that day.

Reluctantly they rose from their chairs and left her office. Alex realised they would have to find even more evidence to bring Dumal down. It seemed impossible, but he had to try.

CHAPTER 32

Brutus couldn't afford to make a single mistake. So he had to be sure he wouldn't be interrupted by anyone visiting the old hairdresser shop, nor the floor above it.

His shooting floor.

He rang the agent advertising the commercial property and asked if there had been much interest.

"Absolutely none" was the curt reply. With the economy so bad and commercial rents in that area so high it would be a challenge for any business to survive.

When Brutus then enquired about the property above, the agent said he had no idea who owned it but that it had been empty for several years. Its worn-down state wasn't helping their efforts to find a business to let the downstairs either.

Good enough, thought Brutus, putting the phone back on the receiver just as the agent was rebeginning his sales patter. Good enough.

CHAPTER 33

Once Alex and Thérèse had left Eloise's office, she ordered Dumal into it.

"What the fuck are you up to this time?" she shouted at him before he had even sat down. I've just had Marie Deschamps lawyer in here making all kinds of accusations about you. Sexual harassment, attempted rape, illegal interrogation of her partner. Please tell me none of it is true."

"None of it is true."

"Very funny César and I wish I could believe you. But we can't have any scandals like this. It could mean very difficult questions for both of us to answer."

"Don't worry, there won't be any problems."

"So you have done something?" said Eloise, her head in her hands.

"I may have acted a little beyond accepted limits with Mrs Deschamps, Eloise, but nothing that she can prove. And nothing compared to, for example, selling class A drugs."

Eloise shook her head, sadly.

"I knew you'd call in your favour someday, and I guess that's today. I've already told them the evidence they have is insufficient for me to take things further, but I can't protect you any longer. Consider my debt to you repaid."

Dumal got up and leant toward her.

"I'm afraid not Eloise. Your debt to me is repaid when I say it is. I know they have nothing that can prove any of their allegations, so tell me how you think you have protected me."

"Because I already have enough to ask Internal Affairs to investigate you. They might find nothing and clear you, but you'd almost certainly be suspended during their investigation. And whatever the outcome, there would be a stain on your character that would certainly hinder your career. No smoke without fire and all that."

"And I could make sure your son is assigned to patrol the most dangerous areas of Paris. I believe he's now a police cadet?"

Dumal smirked as Eloise glared at him.

"You really are a piece of work, César," she said bitterly. "What's it going to take for you to leave my son alone? I've thanked you many times for how you helped us, but I can't keep covering up your indiscretions."

"Just one more thing will do, Eloise. Keep Marie's lawyer off my back. I'll sort out the rest. Legally, of course."

He stood up and left the room.

Eloise watched him as he walked out. For all he'd done for her and her son, she despised him. He was a loose cannon that could easily backfire and destroy everything she had achieved. She didn't doubt he'd physically and mentally abused his ex-wife. She'd gone out with people like him before and knew the ways they used to control their partners.

But she was also a mother. And a mother's love for her son is the strongest love of all.

She'd help him this one last time.

CHAPTER 34

Just like the day before, Thérèse and Alex returned to Marie's home deeply frustrated.

"I just don't understand this," he said angrily. "How much more do they need to at least start an investigation?"

"I'm actually not surprised," said Marie with resignation. "The police always look after the police. It's the same all over the world. Hopefully he'll get a dressing down from Eloise and back off. That's the most likely outcome and all we really want. If he ends up facing serious charges God only knows how he would react."

"So we're just going to let him get away with attacking you?"

"No. We're going to get him to stay away from us if he wants to keep his job. It's the best result for both sides."

Alex wanted to believe her, but deep down he knew this was the least likely of outcomes.

"Anyhow, help me prepare for tonight. I don't want Dumal spoiling another evening of ours."

They had invited a small group of Marie's friends over for some drinks, food and music. They were all involved in the cultural life of Paris to a greater of lesser degree.

Antoine was a musician who wanted to be the next Jacques Brel, the great Belgian singer and songwriter. He had brought his guitar and played some of his own compositions to the general acclaim of the group.

Dio was a fashion designer whose aim was to set up a boutique in the Rue de Rivoli, where retro clothes shops stood side by side with some of the city's most exclusive boutiques. She already had a pop up shop that was a favourite in the city's famous flea market.

She had made Marie a beautiful lace shawl, a tribute to the Vermeer painting she knew Marie loved so much and had indeed viewed many times with her. Alex smiled to see her try it on and her face light up, just as it had at the museum when they had first met.

Philippe was the most successful among them, a photographer whose work had already been featured in several prominent magazines and galleries. He was now working on a new commission from the prestigious Polka Gallery, a series of photographs displaying Parisian street life in its many different forms. His excitement about the project and his belief in himself reminded Marie of her own high hopes when she had travelled to Paris all those years beforehand. She dearly hoped he would be the success he deserved to be.

Finally there was Colette, an aspiring writer Alex loved to discuss literature with. They'd recommend books to each other, her rhapsodising about André Malraux and Jean Genet, and Alex about the stories of Ian McEwan and J G Ballard.

Eventually the conversation turned to their problems with a senior French detective and how his boss had defended him. Their stunned faces when Alex recounted Dumal's behaviour with Marie reassured them that they weren't crazy to worry about what he might do next.

"If the police won't do anything, you're going to have to stop him yourself," said Dio. Do you have enough evidence to expose him in the press? I'm sure Le Monde or Paris Match would love a juicy story about corruption in the Paris Police."

This wasn't something that had occurred to them, but the more they thought about it, the more plausible it sounded.

"Just playing Devil's advocate," Colette said, "if you don't have enough proof, as his superior claims, surely you'd be opening yourself up to being sued for slander. And the courts are very likely to find in favour of a senior policeman than you."

They had to agree this was true.

When the guests had left, Alex told Marie that if Dumal caused them any more problems he would start to follow him to see if he could get firm evidence of him doing anything else outside the law. Something he couldn't wriggle out of this time.

'No, don't be crazy, Alex. He could really hurt you, or worse."

"Don't worry, my love. Thérèse is convinced he'll back off now. But what else can we do if he tries to interfere yet again in their lives.

They didn't have to wait long to see that he would.

CHAPTER 35

Brutus was as happy as he had been in many years. He was sitting in Pascal's apartment, telling him about his plan to get revenge, right down to its goriest details. He said he needed Pascal's help in the matter. Of course, Pascal had agreed.

They had met and grown up together in an orphanage in Senegal, victims of the devastation caused across Africa by the AIDS epidemic. Within a couple of weeks of meeting each other, they were inseparable.

The orphanage was a filthy place where the weakest children were the most neglected and the strongest sold as a commodity. There was plenty of demand for child soldiers to join various rebel groups, while pretty girls as young as 12 were always needed to refill the whorehouses of Dakar.

The kids they couldn't sell farmed the land from dawn to dusk in return for a meagre breakfast and weak soup each night. It was sustenance they most likely wouldn't have found elsewhere, with no parents to feed and shelter them. But it still wasn't enough for the backbreaking work they had to do.

Every month or so, the weakest, sickest and most emaciated children were put in a truck at night. In the morning the truck had returned, but not the children. Those that remained imagined all kind of things, but no-one knew for sure what their fate had been.

The orphanage director had no qualms about selling the strongest children to the highest bidders. The money he made, a little of it at least, was used to ensure the orphanage could continue to operate.

This was no act of charity. He and his wife realised this was the opportunity of a lifetime, an endless stream of parentless children coming through their doors, in a country without the resources to check on their wellbeing.

The local authorities gave small grants to the Director to run the orphanage too, which were mostly returned to them in the form of bribes and gifts to ensure the orphanage was never inspected. The farming work provided just about enough food to keep the place self-sufficient, the weak feeding the strong until the strong could be sold.

Brutus and Pascal were strong. So normally they would have been conscripted into a rebel army, where they would almost certainly have been killed in a futile battle in a never-ending war. Their fate, however, was to be very different.

The orphanage director had been made a generous offer by a Senegalese drug crew in Paris to supply two strong and agile boys to work as drug runners in the streets for them. So the two adolescents soon found themselves running between many of the dealers on the Rue St. Denis. This meant either resupplying them with product or taking the cash they had pocketed back to their bosses further up the chain of command. The only real danger, other than the police, was being robbed by members of other gangs.

Pascal and Brutus excelled at their work, no doubt because they never had any need to prove anything to each other, unlike many of the other runners who tried to act tough to impress those above them, who held their lives in their hands. Brutus and Pascal knew it was never a question of toughness. Any mistake a runner made was severely punished. A second chance was rarely given. A third chance, never.

As a result of being so efficient and trustworthy, Pascal and Brutus found themselves promoted within a couple of years, each now controlling several runners. Every month millions of francs would pass through their hands to the higher echelons of the Senegalese organisation.

When the Paris Mafia had ceded control of the Rue St. Denis to Dumal, very little changed in their day-to-day lives. The Senegalese continued their work as usual, and always paid their dues on time.

Pascal loved this life of money, easy women, free drugs and everything else that went with being a feared drug dealer. It was a life he could never have imagined back in the orphanage.

But Brutus was different. He was growing tired of the endless violence, the dead eyes of the heroin-hooked prostitutes that would stare at him each day and the ceaseless begging of the junkies who didn't have enough money to pay for their next fix. These poor souls reminded him too much of the weakened, starving kids at the orphanage who simply craved enough to eat just to live.

He wanted to go back to Senegal and see if he could find any living relative that might make him feel what it was like to have a family.

He tried to convince Pascal to join him, but Pascal couldn't yet give up the money he was earning, although he promised to one day meet him again in Dakar, when he had made enough money to live there on his terms.

Brutus respected his friend's decision albeit with great sadness. He was pleased that Pascal had, unlike him, managed to put his past behind him. So Brutus had continued his preparations to leave alone.

Then, just a week before he was set to depart for his home country, a shot in his chest from a policeman called Dumal had sent him to prison and shattered his dreams.

CHAPTER 36

A week or so after the party, Marie asked Alex to move permanently into her apartment. He had been spending most of his nights there for several weeks, but it still felt like a big step forward in their relationship. He was ecstatic about this, as he already knew he would never want to be with anyone else but her.

He immediately gave notice of his departure to the Residence Franco-Britannique, who had such a long waiting list that they already had a new student ready to move in immediately.

As he was removing the last few possessions he still kept in his room there, he heard a loud knock on the door. Opening it and expecting to greet the new occupant, he was immediately sent sprawling to the floor by a heavy blow to the face.

He momentarily blanked out, and when he opened his eyes he saw the sneering face of Dumal just inches from his.

"You just had to run to mummy didn't you Alex," he said. "You actually dared to make a complaint to my superior. Now you're really on the wrong side of me, and that's not a place you want to be."

"What the fuck…" Alex started, but the muzzle of a pistol was at that point thrust painfully into his mouth.

"You don't talk, you listen," said Dumal in a menacing tone that made Alex fear he might actually pull the trigger.

"If you make any further complaints about me, you will simply disappear. Vanish into the night, never to be seen again. Do you understand?"

Alex nodded, feeling a blood-soaked globule of saliva running from where the pistol barrel had broken a tooth in his mouth.

"Good," he continued. "And secondly, you're going to leave Marie and go back to your fucking shithole of a country, OK?"

Alex had little choice but to nod again.

Dumal slowly withdrew the pistol barrel from his mouth.

"Goodbye then Alex. We won't meet again."

And then he was gone.

As his tongue delicately felt for the hole in his gum where the tooth had been, Alex resolved to take down Dumal, whatever the cost. Spitting out the blood from his mouth, he swore never to leave Marie at the mercy of such a man.

CHAPTER 37

Alex returned to Marie's apartment bloodied and bruised. She was horrified as he told her what had happened. They talked about leaving together for England, but he insisted they stay. This was her city and they couldn't let Dumal threaten other people in the same way.

Their plan was to ask their friends to help gather more evidence of César's lawbreaking. They invited them all to Marie's apartment to ask if they were willing to help, as well as explain the risks involved. They all readily agreed to take turns following him around Paris, by car or on foot, depending on how the inspector chose to travel each day.

Alex then handed out photocopies of Dumal he had taken from a newspaper front page. As ever it was celebrating the incredible achievements of Paris' best detective.

As they looked at the picture, a puzzled expression appeared on Philippe's face.

"I've seen this man before," he said. "It was quite recently too. That's the Rue St. Denis that I was photographing just last week. He may even be in some of my shots. Give me a couple of hours to check and I'll get back to you."

After Philippe left, they talked about what Dumal might be doing on such a notorious street. The most obvious answer was that he was patrolling the area to note new players working there. But that was hardly work for an inspector of his ranking, and he wasn't an undercover policeman either. So what else could he be doing? They never thought of extortion as this was surely mafia turf where a single cop, even with Dumal's power, would never dare to interfere with their activities.

They soon found out the truth.

An hour or so later, Philippe called. He excitedly told them he had indeed captured the image of Dumal on several occasions while photographing for his new commission. He said Dumal seemed to be taking money from various people, consulting a ledger as he did so. In one shot you could see him putting a roll of banknotes into a leather bag while in another he appeared to be threatening a figure lying on the ground, a gun in his hand. He wasn't wearing his uniform either.

He said he'd bring the photographs around immediately.

When the buzzer sounded they rushed to open the door to Philippe. Triumphantly he held up a series of photos that clearly showed everything he'd described

"My God!" exclaimed Marie. "He's extorting money on the side. Not even his boss can protect him from this. We have to show her these photographs immediately."

While sharing their happiness, Alex still had a nagging feeling in his stomach that they couldn't trust Eloise to do the right thing.

"I'm not so sure, Marie. I don't fully trust Eloise after our last visit. Let's show her the photograph showing Dumal taking a payment, and insist she takes it straight to their Internal Affairs division. If she's still covering for him, she'll tell Dumal instead, and he's sure to try to eliminate the evidence."

"Are you crazy?" Marie exclaimed. "This is really dangerous ground we're entering. And after what he just did to you, I think he really could try to kill you."

"It's not at all crazy, darling. It's the only way we'll know whether he has Eloise in his pocket too. When were these photos taken, Philippe?"

"Last Saturday."

"Then it's unlikely Dumal would think I could have taken them, and he doesn't even know you. Can you make several copies in case he comes looking for them? If he threatens violence we'll have a bargaining chip he can't afford to ignore."

"Of course. I'll make several copies and we can all keep one so he'll never know how to track them down."

"And if he does try, we'll make sure we'll have a set ready to send to Le Monde. It's the perfect insurance policy.

Philippe left immediately to start making copies of his negatives. He said it was quite a complicated process but he'd start right away.

CHAPTER 38

"I've found the perfect place," said Pascal to Brutus. "It's a derelict hospital situated north west of Paris.

"Show me," replied Brutus. It was close enough for Brutus to drive Dumal there in under 20 minutes, but in a spot secluded enough not to draw any unwanted attention.

Pascal drove him to the site. It was originally called the White House Lunatic asylum, although it had been used as a hospital during the World Wars. Now it was abandoned, with just a few rusty old chairs and gurneys remaining in the hundreds of rooms inside.

What paint remained was peeling from the walls in every room. Crude graffiti had been sprayed on them too, but this also was vanishing as dampness spread upwards and across the walls.

The mossy smell pervaded every downstairs room, so Brutus climbed up the stairs to the first floor avoiding the broken steps that seemed to have deterred the graffiti artists from venturing any further.

Brutus surveyed the location out of a broken window. The hospital was hidden from the main road and there were no other cars or other signs of human life to be seen.

As Brutus wandered around the rooms, he was half expecting to see apparitions of past patients haunting this huge, eerily empty place. He could almost hear the screams of the mental patients who been abandoned for life there. It would be the perfect place to film horror movies, he thought, if anyone had the courage to stay in the building for more than a few hours.

Pascal told Brutus to enter the room at the far end of the corridor. It was a padded cell, no doubt left from the days the hospital was an asylum, perhaps used during the war to hold patients with Shell Shock or Post Traumatic Stress Disorder as it was now known.

Brutus prodded the damp padding that ran along all four walls. He then nodded to Pascal.

"You've done well, my friend. Now help me get a gurney in here for its last patient."

CHAPTER 39

Thérèse called Eloise the next day. Clearly far more reluctantly than before, she agreed to see them that afternoon, saying if it was about the same matter they had better bring real evidence of Dumal's misconduct.

Thérèse and Alex again went together.

Eloise was sitting stern-faced in her chair. At least that was before she saw the state of Alex's face.

"My God, what happened to you, Mr Amis?"

"Dumal. And if you had bothered to order him to leave us alone, I would still have a full set of teeth."

"I did tell him."

Alex threw the tooth on her desk.

"Then I'm guessing he didn't follow your advice. Yesterday he punched me in the face, forced a pistol into my mouth and threatened to kill me if I didn't leave Marie and go back to England."

He showed her the hole where his tooth had been.

"It seems you are similarly toothless in controlling your officers, Mrs Baron."

"And you're sure it was Dumal?"

"I'm 100% sure. When someone rams a pistol in your mouth you tend to concentrate on who's holding it."

"And there's more" interjected Thérèse, handing over the photo of Dumal taking money from a pimp on the Rue St. Denis.

"Your heroic officer seems to be extorting money from the pimps and drug dealers on the Rue St. Denis too. You can even see the ledger he's using to tick off the payments. And if you look even closer you can see part of the tattoo on his arm. What would a Police Tribunal make of that, I wonder?"

Eloise's face went pale.

"Is that evidence enough," said Thérèse? Or do we have to take this to the papers?"

"No, no, don't do that!" said Eloise hurriedly. "I'll take it to internal affairs. I'll need to keep this picture to convince them to start an investigation though."

"Or more like show it to Dumal," Alex snorted bitterly.

"That's a ridiculous accusation."

"Is it really" he said to her. Do you really expect me to trust you after what's just happened? Why do you continue to protect him? Why don't you order him to stay away from us?"

"It's OK," said Thérèse, trying to calm things down. "You can keep the picture if you absolutely guarantee that you won't show it to Dumal. He's threatened to kill my client if he interferes any more in this matter, and I'm sure he means it. And you'll be an accomplice to any further harm he does to my client."

"That's a bit dramatic."

"That's easy for you to say. But then has he ever put a gun in your mouth?"

Thérèse tossed her the photograph.

"Here, have it. We have the negatives in any case so there's no point in you destroying it."

Eloise tried to hide her rising sense of panic.

"Where did you get this picture? And are there any more?"

"Why do you ask?" said Thérèse, getting ready to leave. "Given what's already happened, we don't feel safe telling you anything more until César is suspended pending a full investigation. That's the best deal you're going to get from us."

"You know it's illegal to withhold evidence?" Eloise said, trying to put on a voice of authority sharply at odds with the clear trembling of her hands. "If there are more pictures you need to hand them in to me now."

"To quote you, Eloise, we'll need concrete proof that you're doing your job properly before we can give you any more pictures. The ones that are the most damning," Alex said, smiling. "Or of course you can call a member of Internal Affairs to your office right now and ask what standard procedure would be in such a case."

She glared at him.

"Internal Affairs operate from a different location. But I'll bring this to their attention as soon as possible, I assure you."

"We expect to hear from you by the end of the week," Therese stated as they rose to leave.

"Put a leash on your mad dog, or we'll make sure his actions will savage you too. And we never want to see Officer Dumal again. Is that understood?"

"Understood," Eloise sighed.

CHAPTER 40

As Thérèse and Alex drove away from the station in a far happier mood than on both their previous visits, Eloise sat in her office holding her head in her hands.

She was sure that Dumal was guilty of everything they'd been telling her, and God knows how many other illegal acts. Deep down she had herself long suspected him of working outside the law to secure his convictions. Why oh why had she had turned to him when she was so frantic to protect her son?

After she got promoted ahead of him, she hoped he would ask for a transfer to another station, where he would become someone else's problem. That was never going to happen now.

So, yes, she should report him immediately. But, but...

The image of him shoving a pistol into Alex Amis' mouth was proof of how ruthless he could be. That made his threat to her son's career – and even life – highly credible.

On the other hand, if she didn't report him now, she too could face serious criminal charges. And if they really had more damning photographs of Dumal, as she was sure they had, Le Monde would have a field day with the police, and her in particular for protecting him.

Hesitantly she reached for the telephone and punched in a number. A voice answered.

"César, I need to speak with you."

CHAPTER 41

Dumal entered Eloise's office knowing a tirade was coming.

"What did I tell you!" she screamed at him the second the door was closed. She threw a piece of photographic paper at him. Dumal looked at the picture and shrugged.

"What's this?" he said. "A photograph of me walking…" and he made a pretence of studying the photograph more closely. "…yes, on the Rue St. Denis. Is there a problem?"

"A problem? You're clearly taking money from the people there. You can even see the cash changing hands."

He pretended to look closely at the photograph again.

"All I can see is me handing some money to a shopkeeper there. Not everyone on that street is a criminal you know. And it's important that the honest residents there can see the police are patrolling the area. They have complained at an increase of violence taking place."

"Don't take me for a fool, César. You're wearing civilian clothes for Christ's sake."

"Yes, because it was a Saturday and I was off duty. I made it clear I was police, so that the pimps and dealers nearby would worry the street was under surveillance from plain clothed officers. They would immediately pass this information to their colleagues."

"You really expect me to believe that?"

"It's the truth, whether you believe it or not."

"Do you know who showed me this photo?"

"No. Tell me."

"Marie Deschamps' lawyer, along with that boyfriend of Marie's. Alex something."

"Alex Amis," sighed Dumal, grinding his teeth at the refusal of the bastard to heed his very clear warning.

"He accused you of threatening to kill him yesterday too. He even showed me a tooth he lost when you forced a gun into his mouth."

"What! That's absolutely ridiculous. You can check my pistol for any proof of that if you don't believe me. This man has some vendetta against me because of my closeness to his girlfriend. Or maybe it's because I suspect him of being involved in the death of Xavier Deschamps."

"That case is closed, César. CLOSED. I never want you hear you mention it again. I've told them, to calm them down, that they will never see you again. So stay away from them, and that's an order."

Dumal held up his hands.

"OK, Eloise, consider the Xavier Deschamps case closed."

"It gets worse, César. They as good as told me they have more pictures from that street which clearly implicate you in extortion and violence. They're talking about getting Internal Affairs involved for Christ's sake."

Dumal shrugged nonchalantly.

"So what, they won't find anything. That photograph proves absolutely nothing, and I'm sure the others, if there are any, can easily be explained away too. I have friends everywhere in the force too, remember. And above it."

"You'd better hope so, César. Look, I can drag this out for a week or two but no longer. Their lawyer is like a dog who won't let go of a bone. So you have one last chance to make this all go away. Can you do that César? Otherwise we'll both be finished."

Dumal smiled. "I will sort it out, Eloise. Trust me."

Eloise looked down at her desk. She knew what that meant, and that more people were probably going to get hurt. She cursed herself for getting herself into this mess, but this was the only realistic way she could get out of it.

"I'll say you're taking some vacation time if they come back again. Just don't get caught, César," she pleaded. "We could both be out in jail for this."

"Trust me" he said again, telling himself he was right about women cops. They were gullible, weak fools who couldn't act decisively.

Leaving her office, he turned and said, "And consider your debt to me repaid, Eloise."

"Trust me," he says, muttered Eloise to herself. Trust the most dishonest man she had ever met.

For the first time in her entire police career she started to cry.

CHAPTER 42

The day after his second meeting with Eloise, Alex was travelling to see one of his pupils in Montmartre, in the north of the city. It was quicker to take the Metro, but it was a beautiful day so he had decided to try out the new Peugeot scooter Marie had bought him for his birthday.

It was only a 50cc model, as Marie was scared that anything more powerful would tempt him to drive too fast, putting himself at greater risk of a serious accident. This was despite the majority of the city's smaller roads being gridlocked for large parts of the day.

As Alex pooted uphill towards the quarter where the white-domed Sacré Coeur cathedral sits looking down on Paris, he became aware that a black car seemed to be following him. Its engine was running at a low throttle so as not to overtake.

Alex wasn't driving fast (indeed he couldn't go uphill on such a woefully underpowered machine), so he was surprised the car made no effort to pass by him. Somewhat nervous because of this, he decided to turn into a side road to let it pass. But still the car followed him, this time revving its powerful engine.

Alex was now sure he was being followed, so he accelerated as quickly as he could. But he was no match for his pursuer.

The black car sped towards him, clearly intent on slamming into his scooter, which most likely would cause a fatal accident.

To prevent this, he had no choice but to swerve onto the pavement, sending several pedestrians scrambling as they shouted insults after him.

The black car drew alongside Alex, a man looking over as he sped along the pavement. Alex was dodging pedestrians as well as he could, but often clipping their elbows as he went to further shouts of abuse. To Alex's surprise it wasn't Dumal in the passenger seat but a larger, stockier man he had never seen before.

Alex saw him raising his arm. He was holding a pistol, which he aimed directly at Alex. Fortunately there were too many people on the street for him to take a shot.

Until, that is, there was a cross section in the road, with no pedestrians crossing it.

The first bullet whistled past the face visor on Alex's helmet. The second was even closer, hitting the top of it and ricocheting off to smash the window of a butcher's shop.

Alex's heart was pounding but everything seemed to be happening in slow motion. Fortunately his brain clicked into gear before another shot could be fired. He took an extreme right turn into the next street, praying there was no oncoming traffic. There wasn't.

Now he had a chance. He had the agility and knowledge of these roads to evade whoever these people were. He swerved around several other cars on the road until his pursuers were several vehicles back. Then he took random lefts and rights, plus a dash the wrong way up a one way street until he was sure he was free from whoever these men were.

He knew this must be of Dumal's doing, and concluded with disgust that Eloise must have shown him the photograph after all.

He parked the scooter in a dark alleyway in Pigalle and walked back towards where he had come from. Furious at Dumal's latest assassination attempt, he was swearing out loud, which caught the attention and approbation of the people around him. He put his helmet back on to avoid being heard or identified.

Soon enough he saw the black Audi, stuck in a typical Parisian traffic jam, horns beeping and drivers shouting. The driver of the Audi was swearing and banging on the steering wheel in frustration. It was, of course, Dumal. Who the man sitting beside him was, the man who had shot twice at him, was a complete mystery to him?

Alex pulled out a piece of paper and pen from his rucksack and noted down the Audi's number plate. Then he returned to Marie's to discuss what to do next.

He didn't tell her the full story of how close he had come to being killed, as he knew she would insist they leave Paris. He just told her Dumal had been following him and was clearly not going to be stopped by his superior. Neither of us understood why Eloise must have shown him the photograph.

CHAPTER 43

Dumal had hidden his fear well when talking with Eloise. He knew he had to get hold of those photographs fast. And then eliminate anyone that could possibly connect him to his most lucrative business.

Although he'd just failed to kill Marie's boyfriend in Pigalle, Alex wasn't his biggest problem. He would catch up with him later.

He unfolded the photograph Eloise had given him and examined it closely. It had been well shot and developed on high end photographic paper. That was the reason the incriminating tattoo on his arm was so clearly visible. It suggested the photographer was a professional.

But who was he and why was he photographing Dumal that day? Then he remembered that Marie had given him the name and address of a photographer friend of hers when they first met. A man who was photographing Parisian streets. It had to be him.

"Paul? Phillipe? Something like that," he said to himself.

He returned to his office and rifled through his case notes. And there it was, the name and address of Phillipe.

CHAPTER 44

It was another hot and humid day in Paris, so Philippe was happy to be in the relative cool of the well ventilated dark room in his apartment.

He was particularly pleased with his latest shots, looking both up and down the Champs Elysée at sunset. Up showed the Arc de Triomphe with the setting sun framed by the City's famous arch. Down showed the perfectly straight boulevard that led to the Place de la Concorde, its ornate fountain lit up spectacularly as dusk descended for the hundreds of tourists thronging around it.

Philippe was excited. The Collection was really coming together, already far better than he had imagined it would be when he had been awarded the commission. He had a feeling this could launch him onto the international stage, giving him the chance to show the world how he saw it through his eyes.

So engrossed was Philippe in his work he failed to hear the click of his lock being picked and his front door opened.

What he did hear, however, was footsteps on the parquet floor.

He assumed it was his partner Charles, with whom he shared the apartment.

"Hi Charlie, I won't be a moment" he shouted. "Don't eat anything as tonight I'm cooking our favourite meal."

There was no reply.

Thinking this was strange, Philippe carefully pinned the developing photos to the drying wire and left the dark room.

He immediately felt the barrel of a gun pressed against his neck. The steel was cold sending a shiver down his back.

"Take whatever you want," said Philippe, shaking with fear.

"I only want one thing, Philippe. The negatives." snarled Dumal. "Give them to me now."

"What negatives?"

Dumal smacked the gun on the side of Philippe's head, sending him flying sideways onto a couch. Blood was pouring from an open wound on his ear.

"The negatives of your trip to the Rue St. Denis."

"Who are you?" he asked incredulously.

"Oh I think you know. After all, you've taken my picture several times. I'm here for a private viewing."

Philippe recognised the man from the photos he had shown Alex and Marie. But had no idea how he could possibly know about him taking the photographs. Not that this mattered now.

"My boyfriend will be back soon, so just take what you want and leave."

"You'd better hurry then or I'll be forced to deal with him too. And if you both want to live to see tomorrow, you'll hand them over to me now. I want the negatives of every photograph you took on that street."

Philippe shrugged his shoulders. "I wish I could, but they're not here."

Dumal shot him in the thigh, making Philippe scream out loud.

Then he pointed the gun at the knee of his other leg.

"Did you know a bullet in the knee is one of the most painful things a person can feel. And it leaves you with a painful limp for life. If you survive the loss of blood of course. Do you want to be crippled for life, Philippe?"

He cocked the pistol.

Wincing in pain, Philippe put his hands up.

"Stop, stop, please! I'll give you the negatives. They're in my dark room just to the left of the plastic fluid container."

"And the photographs you developed from them."

"I haven't developed them yet," whimpered Philippe.

This time Dumal shot him in the knee. Philippe rolled off the sofa screaming in agony.

Dumal unfolded the photograph Eloise had given him and showed it to Philippe.

"So many lies, Philippe. This is the one you gave to Marie and Alex, who in turn showed it to my boss. She wasn't very happy with me. And I'm not at all happy with you. So I need the prints and negatives of all of them."

Then he aimed the pistol at Philippe's face.

Phillipe winced, but said nothing.

Dumal moved the gun barrel until it was almost touching his eye.

"I don't like being messed around, Philippe. So this is your last chance."

"OK, OK, all the printouts are at Marie's," he sobbed. "We only showed one to your boss because we guessed she was protecting you. The negatives really are where I said they are. Please, I need an ambulance."

"In a minute Phillipe. I just need to check you're not lying again."

The negatives were exactly where Philippe had said. Dumal held them up to the light in the living room to double check.

"You have been a busy boy, haven't you Philippe?"

"Please, call me an ambulance."

"There's no need."

Philippe knew exactly what that meant. Dumal could never let him live after all this.

Despite the excruciating pain, he beckoned Dumal over to him. Dumal bent down to hear his words.

"What side of the street are you on in that photograph?"

Dumal looked puzzled. He held up the folded photograph and looked at it.

"The left."

"Doesn't that strike you as strange?"

"Should it?"

"Yes. Because you were actually on the other side of the street. When you want to copy a negative, you first make what's called an interpositive. This reverses the image."

"And?"

"That means the picture you're holding isn't a print developed from the negatives. We guessed we needed some insurance given what you've already done."

Dumal hurriedly checked the negatives, although he knew what Philippe has said must be right.

Philippe let out a laugh that made him wince with pain.

"So you see I've been even busier than you thought, Dumal. And it's going to cost you your freedom, you murderous piece of shit. The interpositives are well hidden, so good luck finding them."

"Such a smart guy," Dumal snarled. "But not smart enough to save Marie from a similar fate to yours if she doesn't cooperate. I'll be visiting her next and you can be *inter*positive about that."

Philippe knew Charlie would soon be home and suffer the same fate if this went on any longer. It was something he couldn't bear the thought of. So he mentally prepared himself for what was about to happen, and said the last words he knew he'd ever utter.

"Fuck you Dumal. You're done for and you know it. Killing me will just make things worse for you. But then I doubt you've got the balls to pull the trigger."

Dumal snorted, then raised his pistol again. Philippe looked him squarely in the eyes as Dumal delivered the coup de grace, a shot through his temple.

The truth was he was worried by what Philippe had said, but it most likely he'd hidden those interpositive things in his dark room. So he entered it and set fire to some of the photographic paper there with his lighter. He then threw the paper into a pile of negatives discarded in the room corner.

There was a loud woosh and dark room immediately became the opposite, lit up with flames that almost reached Dumal. Swearing he shut the door and left the apartment.

Descending the stairs, he saw a man climbing up, holding a bag of groceries. He guessed this was 'Charlie'. He pulled the hood of his sweatshirt over his head as they passed.

"Fucking poofs" he muttered to himself.

Chapter 45

As Dumal hurriedly left Philippe's apartment block, black smoke was already starting to pour out of Philippe's apartment. He got into the black Audi and drove away. What he didn't notice was a large, powerful scooter pull out and start following him. On it sat Brutus.

He'd been following Dumal for several days, trying to work out his schedule so he could know when best to strike. But there seemed no pattern to it.

He'd leave his apartment every working day at roughly 8.30 am, but sometimes he'd drive, sometimes he'd walk and sometimes he wouldn't go straight to the office but drive off in the opposite direction.

Several times Brutus had seen him drive to the same residence and use binoculars to spy directly into the living room of an elegant and good-looking woman. Why was Dumal so obsessed with her and her home? And what did he expect to see in her living room? There was also a younger man there most mornings.

Was he casing it like Brutus had with Dumal's apartment? And if so, why would he want to break in? Something important was clearly inside that building. Something Dumal dearly wanted.

It was all very strange. And a puzzle that Brutus felt he would need to resolve before he could strike.

Chapter 46

Unsurprisingly Dumal insisted on taking care of the investigation into Philippe's murder.

He strolled through the charred wreckage of the apartment and approached the forensics team.

"And?" he said to them.

Looks like the murder took place in the living room as there are traces of blood that remain on the floor. Then we can assume the dark room was set on fire. You know how fiercely film stock burns, so the murder must have been committed first.

His boyfriend was able to drag the body out. It looks like he was shot in the leg and knee first, then the kill shot was through the head. The first shot would have incapacitated him, the second was intended to inflict maximum pain. Maybe the killer was torturing him for some reason before killing him."

Dumal nodded his head.

"Check for finger prints. I doubt you'll find everything given what the fire's done, but look anyway."

One of the investigation team walked up to him.

"Looks like a mob hit, sir. Torture first then a clean kill."

"Does the deceased have a police record?" asked Dumal.

"We're checking sir. He was a photographer, and a good one by the looks of what pictures survived."
"Show them to me"

The investigator showed him a few sheets of paper. Dumal had to suppress a smile when he recognised them as Marie's street. He had always believed her alibi that first time he had seen her. It was a shame that she, too, would have to die.

"Is there evidence of a break in?" he asked, just to make sure he hadn't left any.

"No, but it must have been one, unless someone followed him into his apartment or he left the door open. According to the boyfriend, only he and the victim had a key to the apartment, and there's nothing to suggest the boyfriend had anything to do with this. We have witnesses saying they heard several loud bangs in the apartment minutes before the boyfriend had even entered the apartment block. They say they also saw a man hurry out of the building shortly after the bangs, but his face was partially covered.

Dumal swore to himself. Only 'partially covered' meant there was bound to be a photofit of him being developed.

"Where is the boyfriend?"

"He's at the station now, making a statement. Forensics will check to see if there's any gunfire residue on his fingers. Do you want to question him?"

"No, let's leave that to Detective Aubert," said Dumal, making a mental note to steer well clear of the Commissariat for the rest of the day in case 'Charlie' might recognise him from their passing on the stairwell.

Chapter 47

The murder of Philippe shocked Alex and Marie deeply.

They knew it had to be Dumal, trying to tie up every loose end that could link him to his extortion activities. And for some reason Eloise must still be shielding him from an internal investigation.

It meant they were in greater danger than they had imagined.

Charlie and the residents of the apartment block had given the police as much a description as they could of the man they had seen leaving the apartment. The initial photofit picture, though very rough, looked similar to Dumal, who had failed to completely hide his hawk like features. But it still wouldn't be proof enough that he was the murderer.

Marie was inconsolable, knowing she had inadvertently led Dumal to Philippe's door. Alex told her there was nothing she could have done because, like everyone, she had trusted a police inspector to do his job correctly.

And Alex had been right in showing Eloise just a single photograph. She had now given herself away as Dumal's protector, and an accomplice to the torture and death of their friend.

They hoped Dumal would now be sure he had destroyed the photographic evidence from Philippe's apartment. But they had no idea what torture could make a man say, so it was just as possible that Dumal now knew about the interpositives they were hiding separately to the negatives.

They had asked Colette to hide them in her home. Dumal would have no way of knowing who she was and any connection she might have to Marie. It was their main safeguard for when he came knocking, as they knew he would.

They took solace in the fact that Philippe had died to protect them all, and probably many more innocent people in the future. But it was scant comfort. They all knew he had a brilliant future ahead of him. A future Dumal had ended in the most horrible and unforgivable way.

Eloise was also refusing to answer any of Therèse's calls, no doubt buying time for her once prized, now despised detective to clear up the mess he had created.

The stress Alex could see all this was putting on Marie made him decide to end this once and for all. He hoped attack would be the best form of defence, so it was time to turn to take the fight to Dumal.

CHAPTER 48

Alex knew it would be dangerous to return to the commissariat, but he felt he had no choice.

He was going to make as big a scene as possible, though, so any attempt Eloise or Dumal might make to prevent him speaking would be witnessed by more officers they could ever hope to silence.

Alex didn't bother trying to make an appointment with Eloise. Instead he walked briskly into the building, jumped over the commissariat's front desk and kicked open her door with as much force as he could muster.

Eloise sprang from her chair as Alex swept her paperwork, her phone, pens and an ink blotter flying off the desk and into the air.

Two policemen rushed after him into the office, their guns raised. Alex ignored them. In fact, he was glad they were there.

"I'm not armed," he said. "I'm just here to tell your boss here that we know she is a corrupt, disgusting liar – and an accessory to the murder of our friend."

The two policemen looked at each other in amazement.

"Be careful what accusations you make, Alex," said Eloise, gesturing to the officers to return to their desks. Everyone within hearing range was staring at what was going on in her office.

She closed her door and the office blinds.

"You showed Dumal the photograph didn't you! Now my friend Philippe, who took it, is dead. That's no coincidence. And his murder is your fault," Alex screamed.

Eloise was dumbfounded.

"That case is under investigation and we have no suspects yet."

"There's a surprise" he replied with disgust. "You are a disgrace to your profession. I know it and you know it. And I'm going to make sure you go down for it. We trusted you and you betrayed us. Don't you care about how much blood is on your hands?"

"Alex, please," she said as calmly as she could. "We can't be sure it was César. Taking photos on the Rue St. Denis is very risky. Not surprisingly pimps, prostitutes and drug dealers don't like having their photos taken. Any one of them could have killed Philippe."

"Of course they could," he snorted derisively. "Because all those pimps, prostitutes and drug dealers know Philippe's address, I suppose. Whereas we know Dumal does. Marie gave it to him when she didn't know what kind of a man he really was. Why are you protecting him?"

Eloise went silent. There was a tremble to her voice, the tremble you get when someone is about to cry.

"As you requested, I have put Officer Dumal on leave while we consider your allegations. If he persists in bothering you, you must notify me immediately. Now please leave, Mister Amis. You've made your point very clearly. I'll be in touch when we know more about Philippe's murder. And if you try to take the law into your own hands or pull this type of stunt again, I'll have you arrested."

"The law doesn't seem to be in anyone's hands right now does it, Eloise. Just know that if you don't stop Dumal, we will. And that will turn out a lot worse for you."

She pressed a button beneath her desk and two cops entered.

"Please take Mr Amis back to his home."

Chapter 49

Back at Marie's home, Alex thought about how what he'd done in that insect shop had led to all this. And though he could never have envisaged the chain of events that had followed, he felt it was his duty to put things right. All he wanted was to get back to the wonderful normality of his life with Marie.

He decided, whatever the risks, to track down César and find unquestionable evidence of his crimes. Eloise would clearly try to suppress any story about her top detective. So they would have to find incontrovertible proof of their corruption to convince Le Monde to break the story and destroy them for what they had done.

Most of all, they needed that ledger. The ledger that would prove Dumal was extorting money from many of the criminals on that infamous street.

He knew the risks he faced and begged Marie to return to her parents' house in Fontainebleau. They were away for a few weeks visiting family, so she'd have the house to herself somewhere Dumal couldn't find her. She refused outright. Come what may, they were doing this together.

He loved her even more for her bravery, but as he left her home to clear his head, the ominous sky seemed to be an omen of what was to follow.

Chapter 50

There was little to admire in Dumal other than his persistence.

The next morning Alex spotted him outside Marie's home in his car, using what looked like high powered binoculars. He clearly wasn't going to leave them alone and it looked likely he had, after all, got Philippe to reveal where the negatives were.

Alex assumed he was working out how best to enter the building without being seen.

All Eloise had said was that she had put Dumal on immediate leave. But that didn't mean he had to leave Paris. In fact, it gave him more time to pursue them without the onus of a day job to occupy him. He would no doubt still have his service pistol, and if he didn't there was little doubt he could get another from somewhere. Had they played into the inspector's hands?

Dumal was in plain clothes, so it was possible Eloise had told them the truth. But they had to find out for sure. Based on her actions so far, it was unlikely Eloise had done anything other than to order him to continue covering up his crimes.

Alex went to the side of the house and slipped into Marie's Mercedes. Dumal was so focused on the rest of the house that he didn't notice this.

He had told Marie to open the front door to the house and approach Dumal's car to see what he would do.

Sure enough, as soon as she opened the door, the black Audi pulled away sharply. Alex followed from a distance until he saw the car park outside an apartment building in the Marais.

Dumal entered the building, and shortly after Alex saw a light go on through a first floor window. Dumal had changed into black trousers and a black hoodie. Looking at his watch, he made a brief phone call. Thirty seconds later the light turned off and Dumal exited the building.

He got into his car and drove off. Alex followed.

Chapter 51

After his latest dressing down from his superior, Dumal knew he had no time to waste. He returned to his apartment, changed immediately into the black trousers and hoodie he considered his real work clothes, then made a call.

"Jean, it's Cesar. I'm on my way. See you in 20 and be sure to bring the ledger."

Dumal hung up then left his apartment building and got into his car. He headed north and after 20 minutes he pulled up in a small car park near the Parc des Buttes-Chaumont.

A BMW was already there, its engine running.

César reversed in alongside the BMW so the two drivers were next to each other. Then they opened their windows.

"Any problems with the collection, Jean?"

"None at all. Here take this."

Jean passed the ledger and a bag of tightly rolled-up banknotes to Dumal through their car windows.

"I have a problem though, Jean."

"Oh yeah? What's that?"

"Someone took pictures of me doing the collection on the Rue St. Denis. It was when you were in hospital. I'm sorting it out, but for the moment I can't be seen anywhere near there, or near you."

"No problem, I usually make the collections anyway. I can keep the cash safe until all this blows over."

"I appreciate your loyalty, Jean, but they are getting a little too close to us. They're sure to be watching the street and I can't have you there."

Just as Jean was processing what this meant, the barrel of a gun passed through the window of Dumal's car. The bullet it fired blew away half of Jean's head.

Dumal got out of his car, carrying the Louis Vuitton bag that bastard Philippe had also caught on camera. He put on some latex gloves then pushed the dead body of his former colleague aside.

He emptied Jean's bag, which contained his take of the collection money, and emptied it into his.

Dumal took two rolls of the bank notes and placed them on the back seat of Jean's car. He put the gun he'd used in Jean's hand, then let it drop into his lap where blood was already seeping onto his brain splattered trousers. He'd fired close enough to make Jean's death seem like a suicide. He also took a cigarette stub from the ashtray and placed it on the ground below the BMW's open window.

The investigating team would, with Dumal's close involvement and careful prompting of course, conclude Jean had enjoyed a final cigarette before placing the gun to his head and pulling the trigger. The cash left on the seat would suggest this was no burglary — and that if any policeman was extorting money, it must be Jean.

Motive was a problem, but the stress of losing his wife, looking after three children and investigating the worst of the city's crimes could no doubt convince an inquest he was suffering from depression and had taken this most drastic of measures to escape it. That would explain why he had parked in such a secluded spot.

All he had to do then was to pay off one of the lowlifes on the Rue St. Denis to identify Jean as the man who extorted money from him each week. With Jean's fingerprints on the money in his car, it would be case closed.

Satisfied with his work, he returned to his car and started driving away. Then he noticed a Mercedes parked just off the road nearby, but no one was in it. He was half inclined to stop and check the car, but then again he could use the tyre prints of this car to lead the investigation team away from those he'd have left at the crime scene, should there be any doubt about his suicide theory. He drove off.

Losing Jean was an inconvenience, but nothing more. Sure, his kids were now orphans, but collateral damage was sometimes unavoidable.

More importantly, there would always be more ambitious police recruits, struggling to survive on their pittance of pay in a city as expensive as Paris. It would just be a question of finding one as loyal as Jean that he could trust for as long as he needed him.

Chapter 52

Alex had no idea where Dumal was going until he saw him pull into a small clearing by the side of a park he'd never been to.

He cut the engine and let Marie's car roll to a spot where it was hidden in part by the surrounding trees. What little noise he made was drowned out by the noise of a BMW already parked there with its engine running.

Through a clearing he could see two cars parked side by side.

The Audi was Dumal's, so who was in the BMW?

He suspected it would be Eloise, so little trust did he now have in her, but when he heard a voice coming from the BMW, it was obviously two men talking.

The unknown man passed a bag and a ledger through his window for Dumal to take. There was then some talking he couldn't quite hear, then he saw a gun emerge from Dumal's car window. There was a flash and a loud bang as the bullet passed through whoever was in the driver's seat before shattering the passenger side window.

Alex watched as Dumal got out of his car, opened the driver's door of the BMW and took a similar bag of money from it. He then dropped a cigarette butt on the ground before returning to his car.

As he started the ignition Alex flung himself down beneath the steering wheel of Marie's car, praying Dumal wouldn't see him as he headed back towards central Paris.

The Audi slowed down as it passed him. Maybe Dumal was wondering why he hadn't noticed this car there when he had arrived only 10 minutes earlier. As Alex was thinking what he could do should Dumal stop and take a closer look, he heard the Audi accelerating away.

He breathed a sigh of relief, then got out of Marie's car. Checking for sounds of other cars or people coming from either direction, and hearing nothing, he slowly approached the BMW. Its engine was still idling, but the driver was going nowhere. He was slumped across the passenger seat, a bullet wound clearly visible above his ear.

Alex recognised him as the man who had been with Dumal trying to kill him in Pigalle. And here he was now, dead, wearing a police uniform. Alex saw two large rolls of 1000 franc notes sitting on the back seat of his car.

In his mind Alex slowly went back through what he'd just seen.

If that book was the ledger from Philippe's photograph, then Dumal must have had another policeman helping him in his extortion racket. This man. And if Dumal had killed him, he must be eliminating anything and anyone that could tie him to the crime. But why leave so much money behind?

Alex concluded this must be some kind of plan to shift blame for the extortion onto Jean, but he couldn't see how it could work.

Dumal was clearly not a stupid as Alex had assumed. But he was a remorseless killer. And now he'd be sure to target them.

With a tissue he carefully took one of the two rolls of banknotes from the car.

Perhaps he could use the detective's own tricks against him.

Chapter 53

Alex returned to Marie's apartment, and told her what he had just witnessed.

He realised how close he had just come to being Dumal's next victim, and how fortunate he had been that the inspector hadn't killed him during their last, painful encounter at the Résidence Franco-Britannique.

At the time he had assumed Dumal's threat was a show of power, not something he would actually do. But the events he had just seen that night showed otherwise. This and the attack on him at Pigalle were Dumal's first two strikes against him. And as everyone always says, three strikes and you're out.

It was clear that Dumal was now rattled though. Alex had to find that ledger and fast. It was the key to proving Dumal's guilt before he could destroy it. Alex had no idea how much time he had, so he couldn't waste a second of it.

He drove back to Dumal's apartment. His car wasn't there. This was good, as he was hoping to somehow find a way to get into his apartment, by force if necessary. Then he simply had to find the roster and the money he'd seen him take from the BMW.

Approaching the front door of the apartment block, he saw the buttons for all the building apartments. He found Dumal's and pressed it to double check he wasn't in.

No response.

Then he heard heavy footsteps coming down the interior staircase. They sounded too heavy to be Dumal's so he held his ground. The door opened and a black arm extended from it. It grabbed Alex's shirt and yanked him into the building.

A large man stood there. He checked Alex for weapons.

"Who are you? And what do you want with Dumal?"

Alex realised this didn't seem like the sort of person he should lie too, so he told him the truth.

"He's trying to kill me. He's already murdered a friend of mine and today I witnessed him shooting another police officer. I suspect they were partners in some kind of extortion racket."

The man considered this, then nodded his head.

"I believe you, Alex. Many years ago he tried to kill me too. But what are you doing here? You have no weapons so what are you intending to do."

"It's a long story, but I have to get into his apartment to find something I know that will conclusively put an end to his crimes. I pushed the buzzer just to check he wasn't in."

"Follow me," said Brutus climbing up the stairs to Dumal's apartment. To Alex's astonishment the front door was ajar.

"How...?", he started to ask, before Brutus cut him off.

"Look for what you came for. But I can't let you take Dumal. He is mine. We have some unfinished business and I don't want the police getting in the way."

"What's your name, by the way?"

"You can call me Brutus" came the brusque response.

Alex quietly entered the apartment and started looking around. Where would Dumal hide the incriminating ledger? He couldn't see any obvious place until he reached the study. Inside was an antique oak desk that reminded him of similar desks his father had worked on when he was a little boy.

He would show his son how to fix surface scratches, straighten warped legs and replace hinges on the desk draws. It was his way of bonding with Alex, especially when he let his son help him in his work.

Alex opened all the drawers, checked the letter holders and any other niches that might hold the roster. Nothing.

Then he remembered.

Some of the cabinets his father had worked on had a hidden switch that opened a secret compartment. He had shown Alex how these worked, which to a boy as young as he was then had seemed like magic.

Alex felt underneath the work top. Moving his fingers slowly around, he eventually found a small, slightly raised piece of wood. He pressed this down and heard a click from the main cabinet drawer.

He opened it and where before there had been nothing except old correspondence, he could now see it had a false bottom. Removing the upper part of the draw, he saw it. The ledger. And a key. He had no idea what the key was for, but grabbed the ledger excitedly. Alex opened it to see an almost endless list of names, each with numbers beside them.

Every page was meticulously dated. All were Saturdays, dating back over several years. Some of the oldest entries had been crossed out, but there were many new ones. Most had ticks next to them, but there were notes scribbled next to others.

These said things like '20 due' or 'new dealer at No.5'. It was hardly difficult to understand what this ledger contained. All the individuals and businesses listed got a tick if they paid on time, or a note against their name if for some reason they couldn't. At the bottom was a total of the money that had been taken that day. It was a staggering amount.

Alex was thrilled. This ledger, plus all the photographs, would surely be enough to condemn Dumal, but he was intrigued by what the key was for.

He was looking around for a possible door or chest when Brutus, who seemed to be looking through the front windows towards a closed down hairdressers' shop, called out to him.

"We have to go, he's coming back. I can see him parking his car."

Alex quickly closed the secret compartment of the desk, taking the ledger and the key.

It was a big risk to do this, but he and Dumal were playing a high risk game. Alex figured that as it was only Tuesday, Dumal probably wouldn't open the secret drawer again until at least the following Saturday. And by then it would be too late.

All he had to do was convince Brutus to let him into the apartment the next day to continue his search.

This time they made their way up the stairs to hide from Dumal, who would certainly recognise Alex. They heard his footsteps on the stairs, the jangle of his keys and then his apartment door shut behind him. They quietly descended the stairs and left the building.

Chapter 54

Brutus led Alex to the back of the old hairdresser shop. They went through a broken fence then through a back door that led to a first floor space. It was filthy but had a few old crates they could sit on.

"So tell me what you know about Dumal?" was the first thing Brutus said. "I saw him looking through the window of a woman's living room yesterday. You were there too."

"That's my girlfriend. He's been harassing her for months and he's trying to get me out of the way in any way he can."

Alex told him about his attempt to kill him in Pigalle, and showed him the gap in his mouth where the tooth used to be. Then he told him about the incriminating photographs they had of him and how Dumal had killed the man who took them.

Brutus nodded and told Alex his story about how Dumal had framed him and the long years he's spent in jail as a result. And why he would never trust a court to convict him.

Alex shook his head in disbelief.

"So he's been doing this for years."

"Seven at least. And he has friends in high places that protect him. That's why he needs a special kind of justice."

Alex then told him about the murder he had seen that very morning.

"I saw him shoot what I think was his accomplice." He seems to be eliminating anything and anyone that could link him to what he's been doing."

Alex held up the ledger.

This is the key though. It shows the payment each of his victims has to make each week – and his fingerprints must be all over it."

Brutus asked Alex to flick through the ledger so he could see what it contained. His fingerprints would quickly be matched, but not Alex's.

He pointed to one name written in it.

"You are right. This man is my friend and he works on that street. But he says the money is always collected by a tall, fair-haired and well-built guy. That doesn't sound like Dumal."

"That makes perfect sense."

Brutus looked at Alex in surprise.

"That's the exact description of the guy I saw Dumal kill this morning. But if he's the man making the collections then why do the photographs show it's Dumal taking the money, with this ledger in his hand?"

Brutus shrugged.

"As my friend's name is here, I'll ask him tonight about how their operation works. How can I get in touch with you?"

 "I'll come here tomorrow and you can tell me. And if you can get me into his apartment again I can continue my search. I found a key there but I don't know what it's for. I need more time to search his apartment and find out."

Brutus frowned.

"It is dangerous, but I will try. Come here early, around 8am. We'll watch the apartment building. He usually leaves around 8.30am, and many of the other inhabitants of the building between then and 9am, which is when we can slip into the building. You can act as my lookout as I open his apartment door.

"No problem. And thanks Brutus."

"Just remember," he said sternly. You can expose him for the murderer he is, but I don't want him arrested. I have my own plans for him. These you don't need to know."

"That's fine. We are going to send our evidence to a national newspaper as we have lost all faith in the police. It will take them a day or two at least to assess it before they break the story. This will give you plenty of time to do what you want to Dumal."

"Good. The police did nothing to save me from his lies. And I can promise that you'll never see him again."

Alex didn't even want to think about what a man like Brutus could do to someone hardly half his size.

"Until tomorrow then," Alex said.

Chapter 55

Back at Marie's, Alex showed her the ledger. It was the missing piece of evidence they so badly needed for Le Monde to publish the story.

Marie had been busy too. She had gone to Colette's to get the interpositives and then to a photography shop to have them converted back to a fresh set of negatives.

She also had two copies of each photo developed and printed out, one of which she left with Colette.

They now had a series of photographs of Dumal extorting money on the Rue St. Denis, with three sequential shots of him beating down a man with his gun then bending over him threateningly.

Although they'd already seen some of the photos before, it was still staggering and scarcely believable to seem them all printed out in full colour.

This, with the ledger and the roll of banknotes Alex had taken from Jean's car would prove the two had worked together and that Dumal had most likely killed his accomplice.

If Le Monde refused to print the story, this would be a setback, but only for a few days.

With their spare set of negatives they could make as many copies of the photographs as they needed to send to other papers. Le Monde would be the most authoritative paper to publish the story, but also the most careful to check their evidence was real. There were other, more sensationalist daily rags who would be all too eager to publish such a scandalous story.

The death of Jean had provoked a huge discussion about the stress placed on police in the country's capital. If it was shown to be a murder, and by a fellow police officer as they were alleging, the country would be in uproar. And such a shocking story would sell a lot of papers.

They prepared a package that would contain all the evidence they had to condemn Dumal. But the key in Alex's pocket perplexed him. Just what other secrets might it reveal, secrets that could overcome any doubts about his guilt?

It was an itch he just had to scratch.

Chapter 56

Alex arrived at Brutus' lookout point the next day, exactly on time.

"You were right, Alex. My friend told me the dead policeman you described sounded exactly like the usual bagman who made the rounds. But recently, a smaller but more vicious man had collected his money. I showed him a picture of Dumal and he said he was 100% certain it was him."

Alex wasn't surprised. He nodded towards Dumal's apartment.

"How are we doing?"

"Nothing yet," said Brutus scanning the apartment, this time with something that looked like a sniper rifle scope.

Alex looked around the dingy room and noticed a padded case next to Brutus. It contained the other rifle parts. Brutus saw him looking at this and laughed.

"If you have the contacts, you can get anything you want."

"Are you just going to shoot him?"

"No, no. Well, yes, I'm going to shoot him, but not kill him. I will do to him what he did to me. Though prison won't be a part of it."

Alex didn't want to know any more about what Brutus had in mind, so he stopped talking.

Fifteen minutes passed, during which Alex took a closer look at the sniper rifle.

"Are you good at using this"
"Good enough"

"And how…"

"There he goes," interrupted Brutus.

Alex looked across and saw Dumal getting into his black Audi and driving away. He didn't look in any way perturbed, so he clearly hadn't yet noticed the missing ledger.

"Looks like he's heading for HQ, which means we shouldn't be disturbed for hours. But his movements are erratic."

"He shouldn't be heading for HQ at all. He's supposed to be on leave. Maybe he's just gone out for coffee and a croissant. We need to be extra careful.

They quickly headed towards Dumal's apartment building. Brutus seemed to be timing the journey, for reasons Alex couldn't make out. Maybe it was something to do with bullet trajectory, like he had seen in films growing up, where the shooter had to calculate the effects of distance and wind speed on the trajectory of his shot.

When they were about 20 metres away, another resident left the building. Alex sprinted towards the door, making it just in time to push his hand into the almost closed gap to keep it open. Brutus was close behind him and they climbed up the stairs to Dumal's apartment.

Alex kept watch as Brutus picked the door lock. He had never realised it could be so easy, or at least made to look so easy. Then Alex heard a metallic clanking.

Realising the sound was coming from the woven metal doors of the elevators that served such apartment buildings, Alex urged Brutus to hurry.

He was having trouble this time getting to the driver pin of the lock, swearing quietly to himself. They could both hear the lift descending, the metal clanking as it did.

Just as the lift was almost level with them, Brutus finally opened the apartment door and they hurriedly entered. A few seconds more and whoever was in that lift would have seen them, and no doubt called the police with a clear description of the burglars.

Inside, they both let out a loud sigh of relief.

Alex immediately put on some latex gloves and went straight to the office where he had found the ledger. Brutus maintained watch at the front of the apartment.

"All clear, but hurry. I don't want to be in here any longer than necessary."

Alex searched the room for anything the key might open.

He looked behind the paintings hung on the room's walls. Nothing. He tapped on the walls to see if there was any secret hiding place there. No luck. He tried the lock on a metal filing cabinet. The key didn't fit that either.

"Anything?" called Brutus from the living room.

"Nothing" Alex replied with frustration.

"Then check the other rooms."

It was the same in Dumal's bedroom, his kitchen and his bathroom.

Finally Alex entered the guest bedroom. On opening the door he found himself face to face with a framed reproduction of Ruben's painting of Julius Caesar. The proud emperor was wearing the same laurel crown Alex had seen tattooed on Dumal's wrist.

He immediately knew this must be it.

He walked to the picture and gently lifted it off the wall.

A safe was there. A very large safe. With a keyhole.

"I think I have it Brutus!"

Brutus joined him in the room. His hand trembling, Alex inserted the key into the safe's lock and turned it. They heard a click and the safe door opened.

They could scarcely believe what they saw inside.

The safe had 4 shelves. On the highest two were 80, 90 maybe even more huge rolls of the same 500 French Franc banknotes Alex had seen in the BMW. They were wedged so tightly together it was difficult to take them out. Eventually Alex managed to ease one away only to see just as many packed behind them, three deep on each shelf. There must have been tens of millions francs hidden there.

The third shelf was full of tapes with names carefully written on them. Alex recognised some of them, all senior politicians and celebrities in France. What was on them was of no interest to him.

On the bottom shelf were an assortment of different pistols with boxes of the different calibre bullets that fitted them.

Brutus snorted.

"Stolen guns. Perfect for framing innocent people."

Alex spotted a gun he had seen before.

Carefully lifting it up he saw some flecks of dried blood on the barrel. It was the gun Dumal had thrust into his mouth just a few days previously.

"That's my blood," he told Brutus, from when he broke my tooth.

"Alex, you are a lucky man. If Dumal had noticed this, he'd have used this pistol to kill that policeman in the car. Then arrested you for murder."

Alex realised that Brutus was right, and how close he had come to being framed by Dumal as a cop killer. He knew what that would have meant.

"What do we do with it?"

Brutus walked calmly to the kitchen, returning with a bowl, some bleach and some vinegar. He mixed the two liquids in the bowl then using a scrap of cloth he had in his pocket he rubbed the entire barrel with it. The spot of rust disappeared quickly, but Brutus continued his work, going over the barrel several times until he was satisfied it was completely clean. Alex looked on in wonder, thinking how different were the worlds they lived in.

He checked the window again to make sure they were safe.

"Take the money, Brutus said. "He won't be needing it where he's going."

They searched through the wardrobes in the room until they found an old duffel bag Dumal was unlikely to miss. Alex threw the rolls of money into it while Brutus returned the liquid bottles to where he'd found them.

There were so many rolls in the safe and he was wondering if he'd get them all into the bag. They just about fitted.

Before he locked the safe and put the key back in place for the police to find when they would inevitably search Dumal's apartment, Alex took the roll of notes he'd taken from the BMW and placed them next to the single roll he'd left in the safe. The police would find two identical rolls of money, one with Dumal's prints, the other with those of the man he'd murdered. Not that it would really matter if Brutus' plan worked out.

"Planting evidence?" laughed Brutus who had re-entered the room. "Don't you know that's illegal?"

Laughing at this made Alex feel more relaxed, or perhaps it was simply the ebbing of the adrenaline that had been pumping through his veins all morning.

They exited the apartment, the duffel bag more or less dragged down the stairs due to its weight.

Back in Brutus' sniper room, Alex sat dazed by what they had just discovered.

"Just how much money does César need?" he asked.

"Who knows how great can be the greed of people?" Brutus replied, thinking back to the Director of the orphanage.

"Do you think he'll open the safe and see all his money gone," Alex asked.

"Unlikely. The notes were so tightly packed it looks like they haven't been disturbed for a while. Just one of those rolls would last him for months too. Plus I doubt he'll risk making any more collections for a while now he's killed the guy who used to do it.

Alex nodded in agreement. By killing his accomplice, Dumal had unknowingly given him the time he needed to ruin him.

"And what do we do with the money?"

Brutus took two rolls out of the bag and stuffed them in his pockets.

"Keep the rest. All I want is Dumal."

"When are you planning on…"

"Tonight."

Chapter 57

Dumal was in a good mood as he walked back to his apartment. He had managed to steer the investigation into Philippe's death towards a theory that an ex-boyfriend had killed him and it was a crime of passion. This would explain why the killer had started a fire in the dark room in case any of the pictures of the two together might be there.

He'd told his subordinates to check into Philippe's past life, so he could frame one of them for the murder. It was a typical Dumal move that would notch another conviction on his already admirable record, and put another innocent man in jail.

He entered his apartment with a spring in his step and, with the sun setting, decided to watch it with a large brandy in hand.

As he ambled towards the cut glass decanter, he caught the reflection of the sun on some kind of mirror. It came from the floor above the hairdresser shop that had been empty since he could remember. His eyes widened as he recalled the sticker he'd found on his window just days before.

He immediately flung himself to the floor as a bullet whistled over where he'd just been standing. It shattered the brandy decanter which was now gushing brown liquid onto his white, hideously expensive carpet.

Moving slowly out of sight towards the door, he very slowly eased his head up to see if he could spot the shooter. Immediately another bullet flew over his head, this time passing through his living room wall.

Scrambling out of the room face down on the floor, he reached the hall, grabbed his gun and looked out again at where the shots had come from.

He could see movement in the room. A large, black figure was hastily packing what looked like a sniper rifle into its case.

He had no time to waste so sprinted out of his apartment and down the stairs, his gun raised. As he approached the hairdressers, he could hear a noise behind the building and saw the narrow alley leading to it. He ran along this, his gun poised, only stopping as he reached the corner to carefully look around it.

About 200 yards away was a man fleeing along the passageway behind the shop buildings.

Dumal took aim but his service pistol was never going to hit a moving target at that distance. Nevertheless he fired a single shot.

"Police, stop!" he screamed.

The last thing Brutus had in mind was to stop for Dumal, so on he ran. Dumal had no choice but to sprint after him, wondering why the man, despite his huge size, seemed to be moving considerably faster than him.

Dumal fired off a full round of bullets more in hope than expectation that any would hit. He was right, and by the time he had loaded a new clip into his pistol, the assassin had disappeared.

Brutus could hear Dumal's bullets hitting bushes, gates and tree trunks around him. One even grazed his arm before he reached the end of the alleyway.

He looked left and right. The left alleyway would take him back to the main street leading to Dumal's apartment building. The kind of street where Dumal had shot him all those years ago. So instead he turned into the right alleyway that would take him towards the smaller streets of the neighbourhood. It would be a lot easier to evade the detective there.

Halfway down he passed a large, yellow dumpster bin. He hid behind it as best he could and hurriedly assembled the sniper rifle again. He didn't have time to fix the scope, but hoped it wouldn't matter.

A few seconds later he could see Dumal reach the end of the alleyway too. He was panting, looking left and right too.

Dumal spotted him behind the dumpster bin, and started moving toward him.

"César!" Brutus cried. "Come and get me if you have the balls."

"I have the balls alright," shouted Dumal, and I have you by yours now."

He started walking towards Brutus, raising his gun.

About 200 metres away he could see the man aiming a rifle at him.

César wasn't scared. Without a scope, this man could never hit him from that distance. But by the time he had heard the crack of the rifle firing, the bullet had already blown his pistol out of his hand, dislocating two of his fingers. As he screamed in pain, the man ran further down the street, then disappeared from sight.

Dumal was exhausted and his gun was broken. Slowly he walked back towards his apartment, clutching his damaged hand and cursing whoever had dared try to shoot him.

First he checked the area where the first two shots had been fired from, kicking in the door but not expecting to find anything. He knew the assassin would never return there either. All he found was two rifle bullet casings that had fallen between some empty crates.

Gritting his teeth to fight the pain, he returned to his apartment where, biting down on a wooden cooking spoon, he snapped his dislocated fingers back into place.

He knew he'd be needing his trigger finger again very soon.

Chapter 58

Alex drove back to Marie's, wondering what to do with the huge sum of money that was now in the boot of the car.

They decided to take it to Marie's old house in Fontainebleau after all. If Dumal survived Brutus' attack, he'd be sure to check for any addresses they may have fled to. If he found them there, they could retreat through the back of the house into the woods until he had gone.

Alex tried to see things from Dumal's perspective. How greedy he was, how arrogant, how certain he was of being able to kill without repercussions. He told Marie that every option to run from him seemed risky as he had the whole of the French police to help him, until that is the story broke and he would be the one who had to flee.

For now they only had each other. Brutus just had to succeed in stopping this monster once and for all.

Their hopes of this happening lasted less than an hour. As they were packing to leave, the doorbell sounded. Alex ran to the kitchen and grabbed a cleaver from the knife rack. If it was Dumal, he would die trying to protect Marie.

Carefully opening the door with the cleaver raised in his hand, he was amazed to see Brutus standing on the doorstep.

He quickly ushered him in.

"Brutus! How did you know this address?"

"Remember, I have followed Dumal here several times."

"So is he gone?"

"Alex, I'm sorry. I failed."

"You failed?"

"I'm so sorry. He seemed to know the shot was coming and he ducked just as I fired. When I saw I had missed him I had to run. I only just escaped."

"My God," Marie cried looking at the blood on his arm. "You've been shot."

"It's nothing, just a scratch. He shot at me as I was running away. But he came out worse I think. I shot his pistol from his hand and he gave up the chase."

"We have to clean the wound anyway."

Reluctantly Brutus agreed.

"I'm Marie," she said as she wiped the wound with Iodine. Brutus didn't even flinch.

"I'm Brutus," he replied. "Alex has told me about you and your problems with Brigadier Dumal. I'm sorry I couldn't put an end to them today."

"It doesn't matter, Brutus. We have everything we need to have him convicted of corruption. We are sending it to the press tonight as we thought he would be out of the way by then. I'm sorry that you weren't able to take him first."

Brutus slammed down his fist, causing Marie to jump back in shock at the strength he had.

"No, this won't do. If the press exposes him, he'll flee to God knows where and I'll never catch him. Please don't do this now, Alex."

"Actually, I think there's still time for you to catch César, Brutus. You can't go back to his apartment now as he's bound to have police guarding it. We'll have to make him come to us."

CHAPTER 59

Alex's explained his plan. It was risky, especially for Marie who would have to play the hardest part. The part only a good actress could play.

"I'm ready," she said. "But we have to get Thérèse to agree too. She's the one who could be in even more danger than me. And what about Brutus?"

"I will not fail a second time" he promised.

Alex nodded and they called Thérèse. She readily accepted saying even Dumal wouldn't be stupid enough to kill a lawyer in the process of trying to prosecute him.

They all met at Marie's and rehearsed their parts. Everyone had their worries as so much depended on perfect timing and their understanding of how Dumal's mind worked. Money was what most motivated him and we would use this to bring about his downfall.

CHAPTER 60

The next day, Dumal woke up with his fingers still throbbing. He had slept with his gun by his side, though whether or not he could shoot it accurately he didn't know. Even the large brandy he had salvaged from the assassin's shots the night before hadn't dulled the pain.

His phone rang.

He gingerly stood up and walked to it, checking first that there was no hidden gunman outside waiting to shoot him again. He saw nothing from above the hairdressers'.

Clumsily he lifted the receiver with his other hand.

To his astonishment it was Marie. She was sobbing.

"Well done César, you've got what you want. You've ruined my life."

"Marie? How come? What's happened."

"He's left me and gone back to England leaving a note about why. I hate you, you bastard."

Dumal couldn't resist a small snort of satisfaction.

"Well I would normally say I'm sorry for you, Marie. But not in this case. I could tell immediately that Alex just wasn't good enough for you. He would have abandoned you at some point in the future anyhow, which would have hurt you more. Age differences like that never work. And he was English, whereas you need a Frenchman to properly satisfy you."

Marie almost wretched imagining what disgusting images were going through César's mind.

"No I didn't need anyone else. I loved Alex, and you knew that you bastard! You know exactly why he left me and went home! You threatened to kill him. And you killed my friend Philippe too."

"You may think that, but it's not true. I've been investigating Philippe's murder and we have a strong suspect we're tracking down as I speak. Maybe we could discuss all this over dinner soon? I'm really not the man you think I am."

"Dinner with you? Never. I'd rather kill myself. I'm sick of your lies, César. But with Alex gone, I want all this over with. I'll give you everything Philippe had that you didn't burn after you tortured and shot him. But in return I want you to agree to stay away from me and my friends for good. Agreed?"

Dumal felt a weight lifting from his shoulders. He gave up all pretence.

"Agreed. I'll be over in 30 minutes."

He hung up, put on his smartest suit and headed to his car.

CHAPTER 61

Marie had already put the interpositives and the printouts from them into a large padded envelope when she heard Dumal ring the doorbell.

It was pouring with rain and she took time to open the door to make sure Dumal got an uncomfortable drenching.

She handed him the envelope through the half opened door.

"You'll understand if I don't invite you in, inspector," she said, her voice wavering with emotion.

"Is everything here?"

"Yes, the negatives, and something Philippe called interpositives. Plus all the developed photos. You can check if you want."

"I will need to" said Dumal, trying to step inside out of the rain.

Marie pushed the door against him.

"The deal is you stay away from me. Starting now. You can check them where you are."

Dumal opened the envelope. Everything he needed did indeed seem to be inside and he could always return if it wasn't. He stuffed the envelope into his coat pocket.

"It's a shame things have to end this way, Marie. But if it's any consolation you got closer than anyone has before. Any closer and you'd have wound up like your poor little photographer friend. After we'd played a little of course."

"How can you just ruin people's lives this way?" she sobbed, opening the door just enough to look him in the face. "Do you have no heart?"

"I even hate my parents, Marie."

He sarcastically blew her a kiss, turned and ran back to his car as the rain streamed down the gutters into the sewers where he belonged.

What he didn't know was at that exact moment a package was inside a mail delivery van. It was addressed to Jean-Marie Colombani, the editor of Le Monde. The paper had broken many scandals over the years but this was going to be the scoop of the decade.

Colette has posted it earlier that day. It contained their copy of the negatives, runouts of the photographs and the ledger Alex had taken from Dumal's drawer.

They had also included a note with the photofit of Philippe's killer and the clearest image of Dumal's face from his photographs, plus details of their meetings to Eloise and her failure to act.

Marie had signed the note, she felt she was signing a death sentence for a traitor. But how else could she describe what Dumal was? He was a traitor to the people he had sworn to serve. They only hoped his execution would be at the hands of Brutus.

CHAPTER 62

César wasn't someone who trusted many people, but Marie's obvious grief at losing that bastard of an Englishman was clear, and all the more pleasing to him for it. It also looked certain she had given him all the photographic evidence linking him to Jean and the Rue St. Denis. Perhaps, after all, he'd let her live.

He had decided, given the circumstances, to give back control of the street to the Paris Mafia in return for the large monthly bribe they had originally offered him. It would take a little longer this way to amass the money he needed to retire from the force and live out his life in the sun-kissed Cote d'Azur. But he nearly had enough already and could use this extra time to erase all evidence of his involvement in both Philippe's and Jean's deaths.

He also had a couple of new extracurricular activities to take care of for the rich and well connected of Paris. These were jobs he had always enjoyed and not just for the riches that came with them. He just got a kick at always getting away with murder.

Summer was his most lucrative, as the rich and powerful frolicked with young starlets in Cannes and Nice, feeling they were safe from the prying eyes of their wives. Until, that is, those wives would receive incriminating photos from an anonymous source.

Alex was one loose thread and César wondered if he should pay him a visit in England. But what could he do from there? And if he dared come back, Dumal's response would be brutal and final.

That only left Thérèse, who now had no evidence against him, combined with Marie's desire to stop any action against him. He couldn't imagine her doing anything but backing down. That meant no more meddling bitches getting in his way, although he swore to himself to do everything he could to scupper Thérèse's career from now on, including tipping off the gossip magazines that she had started seeing a toy boy just weeks after her husband's death.

Once more, he thought, the great César had triumphed over the maggots who had sought to destroy him. And while he hadn't got to sleep with Marie, there would be plenty more women like her very keen to offer up their bronzed bodies to him when they saw his home on the Côte d'Azur.

Life felt perfect again for César Dumal.

CHAPTER 63

Alex had been listening to Dumal from the bathroom by her front door as she talked with Dumal. He held the cleaver gripped in his hand in case anything went wrong. But they had gone perfectly, even though he just about managed to stifle his laughter as he heard the rain pouring down on the inspector.

They were right, too, in assuming Dumal would be arrogant enough to believe his intimidation had been enough to coerce Marie and him and to do as he intended. The rain was just a bonus as they knew he'd be desperate to get back to the warmth of his car.

That's not to say they weren't still scared. Once Dumal had properly inspected the envelope, he might still suspect they had extra copies. Or if Marie had sounded suspicious about what was in the envelope, or anything less than devastated at the loss of Alex, they were certain his actions would have been far more violent.

But there was nothing Dumal could do now to save himself.

Once the Brigadier's car had driven away, Alex rushed down and embraced Marie, swinging her around in joy.

"You are indeed a great actress!" he laughed.

"That was a pure soap opera performance, but he seemed to believe it" she replied, kissing him lovingly.

Putting her down Alex lowered his head and pretended to weep.

"What is it Alex?" Marie asked him with concern.

"Dumal says I'm no good for you and would dump you soon anyway."

She frowned for a moment and then they both burst out laughing.

He hugged her again whispering in her ear, "I'd never leave you for all the world."

"I know. And I'd never leave you either Alex. For someone as smart as Dumal thinks he is, he's surprisingly easily fooled. But hopefully it's the last time we'll ever see him."

"That's down to Brutus now. And how good his aim is."

CHAPTER 64

Brutus was with Pascal explaining what was about to happen, and the route he'd take to the old asylum once he had Dumal at his mercy.

Pascal nodded and agreed it seemed perfect. And if anything went wrong again, he'd be there to help his friend.

They clinked beer bottles and drank to their success.

Then Pascal looked at Brutus, with a serious look on his face. There was a long silence.

"And when this is done, what then? You will go back to Senegal like you had planned before?"

Brutus nodded solemnly.

"To Dakar?"

Brutus nodded again.

"To the orphanage?"

Brutus kept nodding.

"And to the Director?"

Brutus looked up at his friend.

"I will find him. And his wife."

"And…them?"

"Yes, I will find them."

CHAPTER 65

Dumal returned to his apartment on an absolute high. His fears had faded like the sunbeams, which were now barely visible behind the spires of Notre Dame.

He quickly checked Marie's envelope one more time. Satisfied, he threw the envelope into a metal bin, doused it with lighter fluid and set it alight.

As he watched the flames consume the envelope, he could see the first of the photos inside emerge. It showed the ledger in Dumal's hand.

That ledger was a problem. If anyone did investigate him and find it, it would be impossible to explain. But when he ceded back the street to the Paris Mafia they would demand it to make the extortion there continue seamlessly.

He mulled over which option to take, finally deciding to sleep on it and decide for sure the next morning.

CHAPTER 66

Dumal awoke to sunbeams streaming through his bedroom window. Already most of the puddles in the road outside had gone. He felt refreshed from a long deep sleep and felt everything was perfect in his world once again.

He made himself a light breakfast.

He was on a diet, thanks to the extra folds of fat the endless array of dinners had put on his body. These dinners were essential to his work, though. They were how he met the movers and shakers of Paris so he could be there for when they needed him – not realising he was often the reason why. He needed this extra income now more than ever.

He had made the decision to destroy the ledger. It was too dangerous for him to keep and he had to hope the French Mafia would want to create their own updated ledger when they retook control of his street.

Once he'd finished his small bowl of fruit and his coffee, he went straight to the cabinet and opened the secret drawer.

What he saw – or rather didn't see – transfixed him to the spot. The ledger wasn't there.

"No, no, no!" he kept saying to himself as he frantically searched through the secret drawer and the clothes he'd been wearing when he'd shot Jean. Finding nothing, he took the key and rushed to the guest room, wondering if he'd absentmindedly put it in his safe.

Usually he would stand before the picture of Caesar breathing in deeply and imaging himself as an equal to this great emperor. But this was no time for such fantasies. When he opened the safe, it was if the floor he was standing on had collapsed. All the money, that he had extorted was gone. Only two, pathetic rolls of banknotes remained.

Breathing hard so as not to panic, he sat on the bed and wondered who could have robbed him. His first thought was the Paris Mafia, but that was unlikely, despite the recent attempt on his life. They hadn't made any complaints to him in all the years he'd been working the street.

And how would hoodlums like them know anything about the secret drawers on Antique English cabinets?

English cabinets, he repeated to himself.

Surely it couldn't be possible?

But who wanted that ledger the most? Alex, Marie and Thérèse.

In a fury, he locked the safe and hurried out of his apartment to his car.

CHAPTER 67

Thérèse was working on Marie's kitchen table when she heard loud banging at the door.

She knew he'd be coming. She took a few deep breaths to steady her nerves then went to open the door.

She had hardly started opening it when Dumal forced his way into the house, sending Thérèse crashing into the same radiator he'd ripped his jacket on.

"Inspector!" she screamed rubbing her arm which had taken most of the impact. "You're not even allowed to be here."

"Where is he?"

"Who?"

"Don't play games with me, Thérèse. Where is Alex?"

"I assume he's back in England. After your threats he left Marie and returned home. I thought you and Marie had worked all this out together?"

"I'm searching the house. If I find him here, God help you," he said, opening his jacket to take out his gun."

"Show me your warrant, César?" replied Thérèse calmly.

"I don't need one. I'm looking for property stolen from me."

"Not without a warrant," she shouted at him as he ran up the stairs.

He went through the upstairs rooms one by one, emptying cupboards and wardrobes, looking under beds and feeling every mattress for something that shouldn't be there.

Nothing.

He went downstairs again, where Thérèse was on the phone. She was talking to the police and was explaining Dumal had gone crazy and was ransacking Marie's home without a warrant. She urged them to send police officers to come and take him away.

Dumal glared at her, knowing he would only have minutes left to find the ledger and the money.

He ransacked the downstairs savagely, pulling down cupboards and overturning sofas, but again finding nothing.

In desperation he grabbed Therese by the throat.

"Where are they?"

"I don't know"

He tightened his grip.

"Tell me"

"I only know where Marie is," she said, now struggling desperately for breath.

"Go on"

"She's at her parents' house. She's there to get away from you and all the stress you've caused her, you evil piece of shit.

Dumal squeezed her throat harder until she almost stopped breathing.

"Address!"

"On the table over there," she gasped, using her eyes to indicate a piece of paper with an address scribbled on it.

Dumal let go of her and grabbed the note. Thérèse fell to the floor gasping.

He left just as the sirens of police cars could be heard nearby.

Thérèse rubbed her bruised throat, got her breath back then picked up a phone and dialled a number. If anything, her performance had outranked Marie's.

"He's on his way."

Seconds later, two policemen ran through the open front door, guns raised.

Thérèse recognised them as the two who had begged her and Alex not to include them in their complaint."

"He's gone," she said. "But not before leaving me with this." She showed them the heavy bruising round her throat.

"A great boss you have there."

"We're so sorry," said one. "We're not all like him. I promise we'll stop him this time."

"Where's he gone?" said the other.

"I have absolutely no idea," she lied.

CHAPTER 68

Dumal drove recklessly through the streets of Paris. He wasn't even sure if Marie had his money and the ledger, but he had to find out.

It was mid-morning now and the traffic was light. He sped southwest to reach the A6 motorway that led directly to Fontainebleau.

As he drove he frantically tried to work out what to do.

He couldn't call for police back up after Thérèse's call. The police would already be looking for him. That was smart on her behalf, he had to concede. Nor could he kill her. That was a step too far, and would almost certainly see him jailed for life, or as long as an officer like him would survive in a jail where there were certain to be inmates with serious grudges against him.

He decided his best plan was to scare Marie. He'd claim the money and ledger belonged to the French Mafia. If she didn't return it they'd torture and kill her and all her family, then do the same to Alex and his family. Was it worth so much pain just to ruin his career?

Yes, that would work. She was only a woman after all, and he'd always got the better of them.

He practised the words he'd use again and again as he made what was normally a 70 minute journey to Fontainebleau in just 55 minutes.

He screeched to a halt in front of the address he'd taken from Marie's home. It was a traditional country retreat that reminded him of the home he'd grown up in, with parents who criticised everything he ever did. Leaping out of the car, gun in hand, he ran to the front door, shot the lock and kicked it in.

CHAPTER 69

Although they were expecting him, Dumal's arrival was always something to be feared. Who knows what he would do, they thought, especially now he'd been pushed into a corner?

All they knew that this was the endgame, and there could be only one winner.

Marie was in the kitchen, looking startled at Dumal's violent entrance. Her eyes widened with fear as she saw his gun.

"You said you'd stay away from me inspector."

"You said you'd given me all the evidence. That isn't true is it Marie?"

"I don't know what you mean. I gave you everything Phillipe gave to me."

"I'm not talking about the negatives. Where's the ledger?"

"What ledger?"

"Don't play any more games with me."

"Let me think," she said. Then, looking over Dumal's shoulder into the trees behind him, she said, "Oh, you don't mean that ledger, do you?"

Dumal span round to see Alex holding the ledger and a large duffel bag Dumal recognised from his apartment. He was standing on one of the smaller boulders that were scattered through the forest.

"Are you looking for this, César?" he laughed, holding up a ledger book. "Or this?" he said holding up a wad of banknotes.

Dumal fired at him just as Alex was jumping down from the boulder, the bullet passing right where he had been standing. César winced in pain from pulling the trigger.

"I'll deal with you when I get back, Marie."

Dumal ran outside the house to where he had seen Alex.

From further inside the forest he heard his voice again. "That was a good shot Dumal, you're not as incompetent as you seem."

"You are though. This forest is perfect for burying dead bodies. I'll make sure you and Marie can lie together here for eternity."

"I doubt you can get the better of me, César. History should tell you that when the French fight the English they rarely come out on the winning side."

Alex knew how this would infuriate Dumal, and true to form he could hear Dumal giving chase, smashing the way through the foliage like a madman.

Alex could hear him panting the further he ran into the trees.

Then Alex stopped.

As the sound of his footsteps on the forest floor stopped, so did Dumal's.

Alex was hiding behind a large boulder not more than 50 metres from Dumal.

"You're no Emperor are you, César, you fat fuck. You're just one of life's failures who's ready to kill and threaten people for money you're too lazy to earn yourself."

"Show yourself if you want to live."

"No. You've made it all too clear what you'll do to me and Marie. And you'll forgive me for not trusting a conniving liar like you. Drop your pistol and we could fight it out like men, but I suspect you'll be too scared. I'm bigger than you, but then who isn't?"

This infuriated Dumal even further who was now trying to quietly outflank Alex.

As he approached the boulder from the left side, he could see no sign of Alex. He must have retreated further into the forest, the coward.

But he did see the duffel bag lying on the ground. He looked around for where Alex might be hidden and, seeing nothing, slowly opened the zip. Inside was just a bundle of old magazines and an empty ledger Alex had bought that morning. Attached to it on a post-it note were three words.

"Et tu Brute?"

Then Dumal heard a crack and felt himself being thrown back into the boulder. Blood was gushing out through a wound below his shoulder.

His gun had been thrown a few metres from where he lay, and César started to crawl towards it.

"I wouldn't do that Dumal," said a voice that clearly wasn't Alex's but that Dumal recognised from the day before.

Brutus jumped down from the rock he'd been positioned at, still holding his rifle. As he approached Dumal he shot a hole through the inspector's hand to make sure the gun would remain where it lay.

"Fuck!", screamed Dumal. "Don't you know who I am?"

He stared at Brutus. In his eyes he saw a steely look scarier than anything he had seen in all the murderers he had faced.

Brutus approached the stricken man.

"Oh I know who you are, César Dumal. But do you remember me?" said Brutus.

Dumal shook his head, wincing in pain.

"You should. After all, you sent me to jail for 12 years for a crime I'm sure you committed."

Dumal vaguely remembered the case but what excuse could he make?

"I'm sorry, I was forced..." he started.

"It's too late for any more of your bullshit now," said Brutus, pressing his foot into the gaping wound below Dumal's shoulder.

Dumal screamed in agony.

Then he saw Alex approaching.

"How, what...?" started Dumal, his mind scrambling to understand the connection between the two men.

"Did you really think your past wouldn't catch up with you?" said Alex. "Well it has now and you're going to pay for all the pain you've caused to innocent people. And I think it's going to hurt."

Then he bent down bent down until his mouth was by Dumal's ear.

"This really is goodbye, César. But before my friend here takes you away, I have one last thing I want you to hear."

Dumal's eyes flickered over to his.

"A beetle."

"What?"

"A beetle. That was the missing insect you were looking for in Xavier's shop. A big black and white beetle. You were right. I did kill him. But even the great César Dumal couldn't prove it."

Fury flashed one final time in Dumal's eyes. But not for long. Brutus poured chloroform onto a handkerchief and thrust it over Dumal's nose.

They stood up, smiling, and embraced each other as Pascal approached, also carrying a rifle. Like so many of his victims, Dumal has been given no chance. The moment he stepped into the forest he was a dead man.

Brutus hauled Dumal's unconscious body onto his shoulders, like a hunter might with a deer he had shot. They returned the way they had come.

When they reached Marie's parents' house she rushed out and embraced Alex, while Brutus and Pascal threw Dumal into the boot of his black Audi.

"Farewell my friend," Brutus called over.

"Goodbye Brutus" said Alex. "By the way, is that really your name?"

Brutus laughed.

"No. But if you want to know what it is, come to see me in Senegal. In a few years though, once all this is old news."

"How will I find you?"

"Go to Dakar and ask to be taken to the orphanage. You'll find me there."

With a final wave he got into the car and drove away.

"Is Dumal really dead?" Marie asked.

"Not yet," Alex said. But I suspect he soon will be."

CHAPTER 70

The next day, all hell broke loose across France. But nowhere more so than in the Paris Police Prefecture.

Le Monde's front page had broken the story.

CORRUPTION AT HEART OF PARIS POLICE

There alongside was the picture of Dumal holding the ledger in the Rue St. Denis, and beside it a close-up photograph of one of its pages.

Brigadier Dumal suspected of running a protection racket it was captioned.

Eloise Baron resigns, charges likely to follow proclaimed another headline, with a picture of Dumal's boss leaving the commissariat in handcuffs, her head covered with her coat.

Dumal on the run, suspected of murder was the most satisfying story of all. The report said they had searched his home finding a stash of unregistered guns and a roll of banknotes carrying the fingerprints of the recently murdered policeman.

Over the days that followed, the story got bigger and bigger. Two junior police officers had come forward to testify about the rumours of Dumal's illegal activities and the threats he had used to coerce them.

They said he stood for everything bad about the police and the oath they had sworn to uphold justice. They said they felt they only now could come forward on behalf of all the honest police whose reputation Dumal had done so much to despoil.

Over the next few weeks the guns found in Dumal's safe were tracked back to ballistic reports going back several years. This led to the release of over 20 innocent people he had framed. These included Brutus, who was given a full pardon, although he had apparently disappeared completely since his release from prison.

The man who had once been lauded as Paris' greatest detective was now a pariah in the city he felt he had owned.

Eloise was charged as an accessory to murder. She came clean about her son and why she had helped shield Dumal, saying she had no idea it would lead to the murder of Philippe. In return for her cooperation, she received a lighter sentence and her son wasn't dismissed from the force. In fact, thanks to her evidence many new charges were added to the already long list Dumal faced.

It was everything Alex and Marie had hoped for, and more.

Philippe's death became the symbol of what could happen when the police were allowed to act as they wanted, without proper controls. The papers described his murder as that of an innocent victim who had been killed for trying to bring a corrupt cop to justice. He was posthumously awarded a medal of valour. The photos he had taken that Dumal hadn't destroyed were exhibited all over France to an acclaim he had always hope for in life.

Dumal's disappearance was of course seen as an obvious flight from justice. This seemed to be confirmed when his Audi was found abandoned at Orly Airport. Everyone assumed he was on the run with the money he had extorted, probably heading for a country with no extradition treaty with France.

The dignitaries he had lied and murdered for didn't escape justice either. Under questioning most insisted, as these people always do, that they had at most only spoken to Dumal occasionally at various social events. But when they were played the tapes of their conversations with him, most changed their stories in return for shorter sentences. The magistrate who had paid Dumal to kill his wife was one exception. He pleaded not guilty, claiming their conversation was not incriminating, and was jailed for 20 years.

Dumal was finally out of their lives, leaving Marie and Alex to live the life they yearned for.

CHAPTER 71

Dumal awoke with a splitting headache and an intense throbbing in his shoulder. It had been bandaged to stem the flow from the bullet Brutus had fired through him. Brutus had aimed a little higher than Dumal had with him, ensuring a non-fatal injury.

He didn't deserve a merciful death and he wasn't going to get one.

Dumal was attached to a gurney, his feet shackled to the side bars by handcuffs.
An intense pain came from his mouth, where he felt what he assumed was a gag had been forced. He spat it out despite the excruciating pain it caused, only to see in horror that it was his tongue. It had been cut off with a bloodied pair of rusty shears he could just about see on a side table, then forced back in his mouth. He screamed but all that came out of his mouth was a muffled gurgling sound.

Much clearer was the voice of the man who had shot him in the forest.

"Did you know, César, that in mediaeval times, the tongues of liars were cut out. And your lies meant I was sentenced to 12 years in prison, didn't they César?

Dumal saw another man circling around him as Brutus spoke. He recognised him as one of his clients on the Rue St. Denis.

"And thieves had their hands cut off," said Pascal as he took one of Dumal's arms and held it flat on an old hospital side table. "And how many people's freedom have you stolen?"

Dumal's eyes widened in horror. He tried to beg for mercy but just spat out more blood from his mouth.

Brutus brought a machete down hard, severing Dumal's left hand and causing him to scream in a new silent agony. It was then he saw that tourniquets had been applied to both his arms to prevent him bleeding to death.

"Your hands placed fake evidence to condemn me and many others too" continued Brutus, walking slowly around the gurney, watched in terror by Dumal as he traced the machete blade slowly up his body."

He lifted it and this time severed Dumal's right hand, the blade cutting through his beloved tattoo.

As his body writhed in pain, Brutus pulled up a chair so Dumal could hear him.

"The seven years I spent in jail made me think about why people like you do what you do. You use the power you are given, not to help people as you should, but to exploit them for your personal gain. You put me in prison because you had the power to shoot and frame an innocent man. Just for money.

"In prison I saw many people like you. The stronger inmates who used their power to control and abuse the weaker ones with punches, kicks, stabbings and rapes. I saw how prison guards had the power to control these strong inmates with harsh beatings when they overstepped the mark. And how they were controlled by gangs outside the prison who would kill their families if they didn't smuggle in drugs to their friends. So it goes on, the higher and higher you go up through our society. But you know all this."

"So let me tell you something else. When my friend Pascal here and I were children, we grew up in an orphanage, where every aspect of our life was controlled by two people as evil as you. They sold children like us as objects not humans, even though they had the power to help us."

Dumal was in too much agony to properly take in what Brutus was saying, but still the man continued.

"I came to realise that everything in life is about power, César. The only decision a person has to make is whether to use whatever power they have for good or bad. I admit I myself have used it badly. I sold drugs to hopeless addicts, making money out of their desperation. I've hurt people for not doing what I say, because I had the power to do so. But you? You've used your power to destroy innocent people when you were given it to protect them. I think it's time for this to stop, don't you?"

Dumal nodded furiously, hoping for a reprieve he knew would never come.

"I want to be a different man, César. I want to do good for as much time I have left in this world."

He held up one of the rolls of banknotes he had taken from the duffel bag. "And this is going to help me, so thank you for such a generous gift."

Dumal looked in fury at him, finally understanding how his money had been stolen.

"My dream, in prison, was to arise like a phoenix from the ashes. But to arise a better, person, someone who does not exploit others. Unfortunately for you, I need ashes."

As he was saying this, Pascal was dousing Dumal with petrol from a large cannister. When it touched his open wounds, fresh waves of agony pulsed through his body.

"It is here we say goodbye César. But I promise your death will lead to good. Although nothing can redeem your soul."

Brutus lit a match and threw it onto Dumal's feet. Fire quickly engulfed his body and whatever screams he could muster were silenced instantly as he and Pascal closed and bolted the doors to the padded cell.

Outside the two embraced.

"Will I see you again, my brother?" asked Pascal.

"Yes," he replied. When you get tired of this life, come home and we will build a better one for ourselves and for them. Promise me."

"I promise, my brother."

They embraced again then Pascal got into his car and drove back towards Paris.

Brutus got into Dumal's car, which already contained his packed suitcase, and drove directly to Orly airport. He then boarded a flight to Senegal, never once looking back at the city where had been imprisoned for so many years.

CHAPTER 72

Marie and Alex spent a few days in Fontainebleau, reading the news about the scandal and slowly recovering from the intense stress and sorrow of the last few weeks.

They talked about the future and what they both really wanted. As ever, they agreed on practically everything.

Marie had decided to give up on her acting career and wanted to immerse herself in the true artistic genius of others. They decided to travel the world, going wherever impulse took them.

They saw the Sagrada Familia in Barcelona, the Uffizi gallery in Florence, The Sistine Chapel in The Vatican and the Blue Mosque in Istanbul.

They hiked in Yosemite, went wild water rafting in Colorado and took a helicopter ride over The Grand Canyon.

Then, in India, after a week spent swimming in the warm waters of the ocean at Goa, they travelled to see the Taj Mahal in Agra. Marie looked at it in wonder, with Alex standing behind her, his arms around her waist.

"Isn't it beautiful," Marie said, remembering the first words Alex had ever spoken to her.

"More than beautiful," he replied.

Marie felt his arms fall away. When she turned around, she saw him on one knee, holding up a velvet box with an engagement ring inside.

"Marie, you are the only woman I have ever wanted, and the only woman I will ever want. You are more beautiful than anything I've seen in this world. So please, will you marry me?"

Tears started to roll down her face.

"Yes, yes, yes, of course I'll marry you."

She threw her arms around him and kissed him passionately as the people around them clapped and cheered.

Then they sat down on the concrete bench that faced the palace, silent for a moment.

"About time too," Marie eventually said.

CHAPTER 73

Brutus exited the gates of Dakar airport. Everything seemed different to him after such a long time away. The city had grown hugely, and had modernised to the degree it now seemed as much European as African.

But he knew behind this façade there would still be abject poverty continuing as ever in the hinterlands.

He hailed a taxi and asked to be driven to Rufisque, near the coastline.

The driver asked why he wanted to go to such a place.

"Nostalgia."

The driver sensed Brutus was a man of few words and they continued the 50 minute journey in silence.

From Rufisque, Brutus walked the two or so miles to the orphanage. All kind of memories stirred him as he approached this hated edifice. It was closed now, the cheap red paint on the walls crumbling away, the rusted hinges of the front gate creaking in the wind.

An old woman hobbled by, her head bent down to avoid the worst of the wind blowing off the sea, although Brutus remembered times it was far worse. Of course this made no difference to the Director. They children had to work regardless of the weather if they wanted their bowl of thin soup and piece of bread at the end of the day.

Brutus approached the old woman.

"I grew up here," he said.

The old lady nodded sympathetically.

"What happened to it?"

"It closed about 5 years ago when the Director retired with his wife to the coast. I think they now live in a house near the harbour in Dakar."

"Thank you, madame" said Brutus pressing some coins into her hand. Nodding her head in gratitude, she hurried on, unused to such acts of generosity from strangers.

Brutus walked back to Rufisque and took a taxi to the harbour. He found a hotel and flopped down on the bed, exhausted.

He fell into a deep sleep, but awoke refreshed and ready.

CHAPTER 74

Even after all the years that had passed, the surname of the orphanage's Director remained seared in Brutus' mind.

Abioye.

"Good morning, Director Abioye," they all had to say at morning assembly.

"Yes, Director Abioye," they all had to say when he tasked them to do anything.

"I'm sorry Mrs Abioye" they all had to say as the director's wife whipped them with rose bush stems whenever they did something she didn't like, their skin torn as she smiled in satisfaction at her work."

Their screams were a warning to all the other children to always remain respectful to the two people who controlled their lives.

None of the children knew their first names. But Brutus didn't need to.

He went down to the hotel lobby and asked for a telephone directory. There, he found the surnames of four Abioyes. Three were scattered around the city. But one was positioned on the exclusive Rue de la Corniche estate, where for miles large houses sat beside upmarket tourist hotels overlooking the ocean and the infamous Île de Gorée.

This island housed the infamous 'House of Slaves', which for centuries had been a major trading point for that despicable business. Hundreds of thousands of poor souls had passed through a stone gate there to be sent off around the world to lives of misery and torment. It was an appropriate place for modern day slave traders like the Director and his wife to live out their last years.

As Brutus walked down the Rue de la Corniche he couldn't help but admire the bougainvillea-draped houses that stretched along this most prestigious of roads.

Many had large, luxury swimming pools that almost matched those of the hotels located around them. Most of these homes, and no doubt the hotels too, were owned by drug dealers who used Dakar's large port to export their product to people just like him, to sell on the streets of Paris, London, Madrid and who knows where else.

The sun was bearing down as he walked and, used to Parisian weather, Brutus' shirt was soon soaked with sweat.

As he approached the address he'd been looking for, he saw a tourist shop selling cheap T-shirts and caps. He bought one of both, then placed a call to the local police authorities, asking them to come to the address he was about to call at, and exactly why they should.

As he approached the Director's house, he could hear that unmistakeable voice. That hated voice, less strident now than then, but one that had put panic in his heart every day he was imprisoned in the orphanage, just like the slaves had been on that infamous island he could now clearly see less than 6 miles away.

The house's gate was open, a new Toyota Landcruiser parked inside. From behind it, Brutus could see the Director taking tea in the garden. They were sitting on expensive wicker chairs with stylish cushions, shaded by a large white parasol. He walked over to the front of the house where he saw, for the first time, their real names.

Malick and Marieme Abioye stated the engraved plaque by the entrance gate.

Brutus walked back to the open gate, then slowly up to the couple, causing the Director's wife to jump up in alarm. But the Director motioned for her to sit down.

"This man is our guest, dear. We must invite him for tea and hear the reason for his visit. I'm sure he means us no harm."

Brutus pulled up one of the other 4 chairs that encircled the large glass table until he was directly facing the couple.

"You look well, Ousame." The Director said.

His wife looked at him in astonishment. How did her husband know this man? Did he used to sell the children to him?

"So you remember me, Director? Or should I say, Malick?"

"Of course. I remember most of my charges, even though my memory isn't as good as it used to be."

"Do you remember me, Marieme? he said to Malick's wife.

"Should I?"

"You beat me many times when I was at the orphanage, so maybe you should. Mind you, I was hardly the only one. I have some permanent memories of you."

He lifted up his t-shirt and showed her the multiple scars she had inflicted on her back.

"I see you still like rose bushes," he smiled pointing to a sea of red flowers lining their garden. And isn't it ironic that you can see the Île de Gorée from here."

As the realisation of who Ousame was, she clutched her husband's arm in horror.

"We fed you. We took you in as an orphan. We cared for you!"

"Cared? You treated me, all of us, like slaves until you could sell us."

"But look at you now. You are strong and healthy," said Malick trying to calm Brutus down.

"I was only 12!" Brutus shouted at him, rising from his chair and causing The Director to cower.

"Twelve! Twelve years old and you sold me to be a drugs runner in Paris. Most runners are dead within months. You knew this but did you care? All you ever thought about was the money we were worth to you."

He loomed over Marieme who was shaking with fear and spat in her face. She was too scared even to raise her hand to wipe it off her face.

"That's all in the past now, Ousame" said Malick as calmly as he could. "And we're sorry. But everything seems to have turned out alright for you in the end."

Ousame looked up and around the house slowly before his attention was again fixed on the couple.

"Better than alright for you, it seems. But this house is built on blood. How many children did you sell to afford this? Do you ever even think about them? Do you ever even feel any guilt?"

The couple said nothing.

Brutus turned to the Director, his fists clenched, fighting the urge to beat him to death in front of his wife.

"Are you going to kill us? Please don't kill us," stammered Marieme.

"I'm not going to kill you, though I would love to. I just want you to tell me just one thing Director Obiaye."

"Ok, ok" he said, trying to avoid Brutus' stare.

"Where are they?"

"Where are who?"

"Where are they?" Brutus said again, his voice louder.

"Where are who?" said Malick again defiantly.

"I see time has not softened you, Malick."

This time Ousame put his giant hands around Marieme's throat and she started to choke as he raised her into the air as if she was as light as a feather.

Suddenly all of Malick's defiance seemed to desert him and he slumped in his chair.

"Let go of her Ousame. Please. They're about 5kms north of the orphanage. Take the road until you see a concrete factory on your left. To the right is a large area of undeveloped land. They are buried in a pit there, behind a row of disused houses just out of sight of the road. Is that enough for you?"

"It's enough for me," said Ousame, as the sound of police sirens could be heard in the distance. "But I don't think it will be enough for them."

The director's wife rose in a panic.

"We need to run," she shouted at her husband. He slowly shook his head.

"No darling, we're too old. There's no escape now from what we did."

For the first time in his life, Brutus detected the slightest hint of remorse in the Director's voice. But he didn't believe it.

We knew this day would come and we must face the consequences together."

"But I don't want to go to prison, Malick.

"Don't worry my love, I'm sure we'll be dead before they can convict us. We can afford good lawyers."

"Yes, sit down Marieme," Ousame said. "You need to think how you're going to convince the justice system them that you cared so well for us. I don't think even the best lawyers could protect you from the crimes you've committed."

CHAPTER 75

When the police dug up the ground Ousame had directed them to, they found the bodies of over 300 children.

Many showed signs of extreme malnutrition, broken limbs and other injuries suffered as a result of their abuse at the orphanage. Some of the older girls, 'older' being about 14, had been pregnant when they died. Some seemed to have been buried alive, too weak to crawl out of the pit.

The Director's wife got her wish not to go to prison. The outcry across Senegal was so extreme that she and her husband were summarily tried and shot against the wall of the orphanage where they had caused such torment. TV companies filmed their execution and broadcast it across the continent.

Ousame became a national hero, as he was the only child who had ever returned to recount the horrors of those who had been trusted to the care of the two now most reviled people in Senegal.

When he appealed for funds to level the old building and build a new, larger and properly equipped orphanage, donations poured in from around the country. With an election looming, the government agreed to match every cent raised.

All the assets of Malick and his wife, including their luxury home, cars and multiple bank accounts were seized and the money placed in a trust to ensure there were funds to support the orphanage for many decades to come.

The new building was built within a year and dubbed 'Ousame's Orphanage'.

Ousame promised the nation that he would make it a place of hope for the victims of the AIDS epidemic which was still ravaging Africa.

He employed doctors, nurses and child mental health experts to help the children deal with their experiences. He didn't even need to employ teachers as so many volunteered their help because they wanted to be able to tell their children one day that they had worked with as special a man as Ousame.

As well as overseeing everything at the orphanage, Ousame made a point of talking with every child when it came time for them to leave. He told them about his experiences and how they must avoid being exploited. He made every child promise they would do good things in their lives to help those who had nothing.

His orphanage became the model for many others across the country and beyond its borders too.

CHAPTER 76

Marie and Alex were married in Paris. It was a wonderful day, with all their friends present to toast their future as man and wife.

Thérèse bought her boyfriend with her. He looked vaguely familiar to Alex and she explained he was Patrique, one of the policeman who had taken Alex to be questioned by Dumal that day. Her nickname for him was Tweedle-Dee, after what Marie had first called him.

He apologised to Alex again for his actions that day, saying he was sorry that Dumal had still not been found, but they were continuing to look for him. Alex told him not to worry, and that he could see he was a man worthy of being a police officer and how delighted he was that Patrique was with a woman as wonderful as Thérèse.

When the time came for Marie to toss her bouquet of flowers, they made sure it would be in the direction of Thérèse – and to cap the perfect day she caught it.

Marie and Alex had travelled so much over the previous two years, they hadn't decided where they should go on their honeymoon. They waited for inspiration to guide them. Then Alex remembered what Brutus had told him by the forest in Fontainebleau.

"Let's go to Senegal," he said. "And find out what Brutus' real name is and why he asked us to go to an orphanage there."

Marie looked at him, confused.

"You don't remember? Then I'll tell you during the flight."

Marie remained hesitant until Alex explained how wonderful the beaches were said to be. Within a week they were on a plane to Dakar.

CHAPTER 77

During the flight to Dakar, Alex reminded Marie of their last meeting with Brutus and what he had said to him about finding him at an orphanage and discovering his real name.

He said it had always puzzled him why the man who had helped save them had simply told him to call him Brutus. Maybe it was because he didn't want anyone to know his real name to because it was the perfect name for the person to deliver the final, fatal blow to César.

"Do you think he'll still be there?" asked Marie.

"I hope so. I think he had plans for that place to be so sure we could meet him there."

Marie had only at that point seen Brutus twice. Once when he arrived unexpected at her doorstep having failed to shoot Dumal and the other when he was putting Dumal into the boot of the inspector's car, never to be seen or heard of again.

Alex assured her he was a man who he completely trusted, reminding her how good a judge of character he was, and teasing her that she was the one exception.

As the taxi cruised along the road to Rufisque, they wondered what an orphanage in this part of the world would look like. They had seen the terrible TV footage of filthy Romanian orphanages after the fall of Ceausescu and were hoping this wouldn't be something that would distress them similarly.

The taxi driver asked where exactly we wanted to go to and when they both said together "the orphanage" a beaming smile broke out on his face.

"Ousame's Orphanage!" he exclaimed. "Do you know him?"

"Yes, he's a friend from when he lived in Paris."

"He is a very great man," the driver proclaimed.

They looked at each other wondering if we were going to the right place.

Then they arrived.

CHAPTER 78

As they got out of the taxi and started to walk up the path to what seemed more like a large sports centre than an orphanage, Brutus came bounding down the path to greet them.

"Alex! You came. And you too Marie. But who is this?"

They turned to see the taxi driver had followed them up the path.

"I just wanted to see you, sir" he said to Ousame. "You are a hero of my family. Can I have a picture taken with you, sir?"

"Of course," said Ousame, clearly used to such requests.

From somewhere the taxi driver pulled out an old polaroid camera. Marie took the photo and the taxi driver trotted back to his car, proudly holding the developing picture in his hand. He absolutely refused to take any money from us for the ride from the airport.

"So it's Ousame" said Alex.

"Yes, my friend. How did you find out my secret?"

"It seems you're quite a celebrity here. 'Ousame's Orphanage' that taxi driver called this."

Ousame let out a burst of laughter.

"Yes, they do. Come, come. I will show it to you."

They walked inside a large front gate to be met by the of some children playing hopscotch in a fenced off play area. Away from this they could see other children, immaculately dressed, taking lessons in a classroom. From a kitchen they could smell a casserole being baked. There was also a man refereeing a football match some kids were playing in the main orphanage play space.

Ousame beckoned at him to come join them.

As the man approached, Alex remembered him from that day in Fontainebleau, when he helped Brutus carry Dumal to his car. Only this time he had picked up a small boy who had been playing football. The boy had his arm around his neck.

"Alex, Marie, this is Pascal. The brother I found here when we were young. And this is his son, Benoit."

Pascal embraced them, putting his son into the arms of Marie. They had tried to have children but without luck, and Alex felt a pang of sorrow as she held the little boy lovingly, swinging him around in her arms as he giggled.

"I remember you, Pascal. But I never got the chance to thank you for everything you did that day," said Alex.

"All I did was keep my rifle fixed on the cop when he burst into your home, just in case he tried to kill you, Marie. When he held you by the throat I was about to shoot, but I don't think Ousame would have ever forgiven me. My aim is not as good as his, and I might have killed Dumal before he got what he deserved. Fortunately Alex did a great job in drawing him into the forest.

"This is an amazing place," Alex said. "And so different to how you described it, Ousame."

Pascal smiled a bitter smile.

"That place is gone, thanks to Ousame. Not a brick remains. We have built in its place one of hope for our country's orphaned children."

Marie and Alex looked around in wonder.

"Please show us around Ousame."

"Of course, but why the hurry? You must stay with us for as long as you want. I insist. We have a spare room you can stay in and I know Pascal's wife will be desperate to meet you and hear about our adventures in Paris."

"Just be sure to compliment her cooking," laughed Pascal.

"And you, Ousame. Are you married?" asked Alex.

"Yes, and you will meet my wife tonight too."

"And children?" asked Marie.

"These are my children, every one of them!" said Ousame proudly, his hand sweeping across the orphanage where hundreds of happy children were going about their daily activities.

The gesture made Alex remember the similar action he'd made in the insect seller's shop what seemed now like a lifetime ago. But what Ousame had done was pure good, not on a whim but through a desire to give more children a start in life better than he and Pascal had been given.

Alex placed his arm around Ousame's shoulder, but inside he felt a pang of guilt he had never felt before.

That night they ate alongside Ousame, Pascal and the two wives. On separate tables sat all the orphans, including Benoit who was treated no differently from all the other children.

Everyone had the same food and washed and dried their empty plates and dirty cutlery in one of the several large bowls of hot water placed at the end of each table.

"Ousame's orphanage," said Alex, looking around the building. "You must be so proud of what you've done here. While Marie and I have been travelling the world for fun, you've created all this."

Ousame smiled.

"This is all I wanted. And when I finally convinced Pascal to join me here, my life was complete."

"Is there any way we can help?" Marie asked.

Brutus thought.

"Well, we could do with a French teacher, Marie – and an English one too, if you're interested Alex? The pay isn't great but helping these children more than makes up for it."

They looked at each other and, as if by telepathy, immediately nodded.

"Children, meet your new English and French teachers," boomed Ousame over to the children's tables.

The children clapped and laughed, many rushing over to hug Marie and Alex. They too now had children to care for, and the tears welling in Marie's eyes was the happiest sight Alex had ever seen.

CHAPTER 79

Alex and Marie stayed at the orphanage for many years. Ousame was, as usual, right. The sound of children's laughter is the most intoxicating of all, and felt so much more rewarding than any of the luxuries they could have enjoyed back in Paris.

But still a pang of guilt persisted inside Alex. He still hadn't told Marie he had killed her husband.

One night, after they had taken all the orphanage's children for a barbecue on the beach, Alex remained sitting in the sand, poking at a still smouldering piece of driftwood.

Ousame saw he had something on his mind and sat down beside him.

"Are you ok my friend?"

Alex shrugged.

"Do you want to tell me?"

Alex shook his head.

"OK, but if ever you do, you know I'm here for you."

Alex smiled. Then, as Ousame was walking back towards the orphanage, Alex called out to him.

"Ousame, do you think there's more good in people than bad?" he asked.

Ousame returned and sat down again.

"That's not an easy question to answer, Alex. Why do you ask?"

Alex said nothing.

"A few years ago, I did something very bad. And even though many good things have come from it, that was only by chance. It's just the way things have worked out"

Brutus put his arm around Alex's shoulder.

"In my life, Alex, I've seen and done many things. All I can say is that most actions aren't black or white. They exist in all the shades of colour in-between. The only certainty is that they can't be undone. So don't dwell on the past. Just do the best you can to make the future better. And you are doing that here."

Alex smiled.

"You're a wise man Ousame."

"And I'm good at picking locks too," he laughed.

They got up and hugged, just as they had that day in Fontainebleau. Then they walked slowly back to the orphanage.

Nothing more needed to be said.

THE END

Acknowledgements

Many thanks to Vicky Iveson for her excellent editing and proofing services. And to my wonderful sister Fiona for her constant encouragement. Thanks also to Mark Hill who helped keep me on track when I started writing this book in Sardinia.

Printed in Great Britain
by Amazon